Dear Romance Reader,

Welcome to a world of breathtaking passion and never-ending romance.
Welcome to *Precious Gem Romances*.

It is our pleasure to present *Precious Gem Romances*, a wonderful new line of romance books by some of America's best-loved authors. Let these thrilling historical and contemporary romances sweep you away to far-off times and places in stories that will dazzle your senses and melt your heart.

Sparkling with joy, laughter, and love, each *Precious Gem Romance* glows with all the passion and excitement you expect from the very best in romance. Offered at a great affordable price, these books are an irresistible value—and an essential addition to your romance collection. Tender love stories you will want to read again and again, *Precious Gem Romances* are books you will treasure forever.

Look for eight fabulous new *Precious Gem Romances* each month—available only at Wal★Mart.

Lynn Brown, Publisher

DREAM OF LOVE

Joan Darling

Zebra Books
Kensington Publishing Corp.

http://www.zebrabooks.com

ZEBRA BOOKS are published by

Kensington Publishing Corp.
850 Third Avenue
New York, NY 10022

Copyright © 1997 by Joan Darling

All rights reserved. No part of this book may be reproduced in any form or by any means without the prior written consent of the Publisher, excepting brief quotes used in reviews.

If you purchased this book without a cover you should be aware that this book is stolen property. It was reported as "unsold and destroyed" to the Publisher and neither the Author nor the Publisher has received any payment for this "stripped book."

Zebra and the Z logo Reg. U.S. Pat. & TM Off.

First Printing: August, 1997
10 9 8 7 6 5 4 3 2 1

Printed in the United States of America

Chapter 1

Her nightmares always began the same way, harmlessly, with no hint of the terror that was to come. Tonight Ashly ran from the sleeping cottage and, on trembling legs, sped across cool white sands toward the water's edge. The moon lay hidden behind sooty clouds. Only a soft golden glow shone from globes on the four-story condo that overshadowed Jessamine's white frame cottage set among tall, wispy pines on Sanibel Island.

She slowed her steps, forced herself to breathe deeply and evenly to still her trembling, to drive out the fear and panic that always came with the nightmare. She strained to see, to avoid stepping on sharp shells, skittering crabs, sea urchins, and other creatures tossed ashore by the choppy waters of the Gulf. In the inky darkness just before dawn, there was little likelihood of being seen. The last thing she wanted was to be seen, or to see anyone. Not like this: weak, shaken, defenseless, consumed with guilt.

Though the crash had happened early in December, more than six weeks ago, still the nightmares invaded her sleep with the suddenness of a summer storm. Always about an airplane diving into a dark river, about passengers around her slipping below the icy surface, freezing, drowning. Herself struggling through the roiling waters trying to save Werner. She would awake to panic, then gradually, painfully, claw her way back to reality.

Daytime was worse. Without warning, triggered by some trivial incident, every detail of the tragedy would burst into her mind like an explosion. Eyes closed, hands clenched, she would relive the horror. Strangely, the horror of the flashback was more vivid, more terrifying than the disaster itself.

"Post Traumatic Stress Disorder," said her therapist. "A normal reaction, a way of coping with a catastrophe. All your feelings of anxiety, depression, grief, fear, and anger are normal. It may be months before the symptoms begin to fade, and possibly years before they no longer occur."

Immediately after the crash she had felt numb. It was the calm before the storm. The full effect had struck weeks later. Tonight her throat closed on a silent scream of terror. Her heart pounded against her ribs and a fine dew mottled her skin. She awoke with a terrible feeling of being out of control, helpless. Panic overwhelmed her. She jumped out of bed and ran wildly from the cottage.

She shivered as the chill night breeze swept through the thin fabric of her white shortie gown and prickled her arms and shoulders. She breathed deeply of the bracing salt-sea air, listened to the rush of waves lapping upon the shore, their faint echo as they dashed away. Velvet sand gave way to a shining, hard-packed surface. At the water's edge, she stopped short. Sternly she reminded herself that she had always loved to swim—before the crash.

She clenched her fists and forced herself to take one step, then another, and another. Water eddied about her ankles, cool and soothing. Gaining confidence, she waded farther into the surf.

A beam of light slashed across the dark, shining water. Startled, Ashly swung around. Far down the beach the white glare of disembodied lights bobbed along the shore. Shrimpers, she thought, returning with their catch, at least

DREAM OF LOVE

half a mile away. They'd never see her in the predawn darkness. Reassured, she waded deeper. Water curled about her waist, puffing out her gown like gauzy wings. Gradually she relaxed, giving herself over to the rocking rhythm of the sea. If only the foam-tipped waves would wash away the pain and anguish of the past.

A flicker of light caught her attention. Glancing over her shoulder, her eyes widened in surprise. The bobbing white lights down the beach were wending slowly toward her in a straggling column. As they drew nearer, Ashly frowned. They were not shrimpers, but shellers intent on finding rare specimens—lion's paws or junonias—cast on Sanibel's shore by the incoming tide. Her gaze was drawn to a bronzed, muscular man clad in red swim trunks and a white windbreaker. He was striding far ahead of the others, head down, scanning the shell-strewn sands.

Ashly plunged deeper into the surf. She sank to her chin, enjoying the tingling sensation of the chilly water creeping up her back, swirling her hair in a golden tide about her shoulders. She tipped her head back, and floating on the buoyant salt water, drifted toward the sea. She closed her eyes and allowed herself a victorious smile. She had won a small war. This time, she had conquered her fear and dread of the water.

What if she submerged, dived down to the floor of the Gulf? Would she surface reborn, free from the guilt and remorse that haunted her nights and days? Taken with the idea, she took a deep breath and plunged into the dark waves. Water filled her ears with a roaring hollow sound. Her hair flowed about her face like waving sea fans. She kicked hard, stroking downward, and brushed the dark-domed back of a horseshoe crab half-buried in the sandy floor of the ocean. Exhaling slowly, she floated upward.

Abruptly she stiffened. A sudden change in the rhythmic flow of the current, or perhaps some sixth sense, warned her of an alien presence. The next instant a long, dark shape darted past her. A shark? thought Ashly, alarmed. With swift, strong kicks, she shot upward, breaking the surface of the water. Behind her she heard a loud hissing gasp, like a sharp intake of breath.

Frantically treading water, she glanced over her shoulder. She was treading nose to nose with the sleek black head, dark shining eyes and wide smile of a friendly bottlenose porpoise. She burst out laughing as he gave her arm a nudge and fishtailed away. A second porpoise surfaced, then another. Soon she was surrounded by a family of porpoises, leaping and diving, as if performing just for her.

Feeling suddenly light-hearted, Ashly tapped one on the nose and darted away. The next moment she felt a gentle bump on her left shoulder. A grinning porpoise sailed past her. Laughing, leaping, diving, she joined in their game of tag.

Somewhere behind her she heard a vigorous shout waft across the water. She swung about, scanning the shore. The bronzed sheller in the red trunks had tossed his windbreaker aside. Waving wildly, he raced into the surf.

"Hold on! I'm coming after you!"

Ashly froze, her gaze riveted on the shore. In the dusky gray dawn, people were flashing lights, pointing, shouting, yelling excitedly. "Here's one! Where? Over here! Hurry! They're sinking, washing away!"

The scene, superimposed on an earlier scene, merged with memory. Terrified shouts and screams echoed in her head. She stiffened her spine, clenched her jaw. This time she would not give in to the horror. *Would not black out!* She twisted around to escape the scene that seared her memory, but all about her she saw floundering black shapes, amorphous faces sinking below the surface of the dark icy water. Agonized voices, shrieking, crying, pleading, filled her mind. Paralyzing fear swept through her. Her throat closed. She was slipping, sliding down, down into darkness.

A terrified scream echoed and re-echoed inside her head. Her blood pounded in her ears. Gasping, sputtering, she became aware that she was being towed through the water. A hard, muscular body pressed against her back.

Knees grazed the backs of her thighs, shins brushed her calves, a large palm cupped her chin. With his free arm, her rescuer ploughed with strong, sure strokes through the surf. The moon slid from behind sooty clouds, cast a gilded silver pathway before them. A small knot of shellers who stood watching, poised to help, moved on, their lights disappearing beyond a bend of the shore.

In waist-high water the stranger gained his feet. With the ease of a fisherman landing a grouper, he hoisted Ashly over one shoulder and with smooth, easy strides waded ashore. Before them loomed yellow stucco condos with red-tiled roofs. Terraces overlooked a pool set in a vivid green lawn, and bright flower beds bordered the white sand beach.

A shiver coursed through her. Her skin prickled and she was uncomfortably aware of her erect nipples under the thin fabric of her gown. He scooped his windbreaker from the sand, draped it around her and tucked the collar under her chin. It hung well below her knees, past the hem of her gown. He wrapped it gently around her legs. Sliding an arm under her shoulders, the other under her knees, he held her close against his chest then sank down onto the sand under a blue-and-white-striped cabana. With a gentle hand, he brushed her cheek, and pressed her head in the warm curve of his shoulder.

She saw an expression of compassion suffuse his features as he gazed down at her. "What's your name?" he asked softly. "Where do you live?"

Ashly tried to speak, and could not. Numbly she clung to him, her arms wound about his neck as she struggled to recover her composure.

"You're okay," he murmured. "You're safe with me." His arms tightened around her.

Comfort flowed like warm honey through her veins. Gradually, her trembling subsided. As if exhausted from having fought through some devastating upheaval, she gave a deep sigh and closed her eyes.

He cradled her close in his arms, as if to share the

warmth of his body and shield her from the cool, gusting breeze. Tenderly he stroked her forehead, smoothed wet strands of hair back from her face, then massaged the back of her neck with small, circular motions of his thumbs. Softly, he murmured words of reassurance, holding her close until the sky paled and ribbons of purple, magenta, and ivory streaked the horizon above the molten gray waters of the Gulf. A bevy of sandpipers scurried across the shining wet sand to meet lacy, foam-edged waves, then scurried out of reach. A wedge of screeching gulls swooped down for a landing and stood at attention facing the rising sun. Without warning, they took off in a flurry of flapping wings and raucous cries.

Ashly roused, gazing up into the face of the stranger. He wasn't the handsomest man she'd ever seen, but his clean-cut good looks proclaimed an honesty and sincerity that inspired confidence. His skin, the color of scorched earth, accentuated a thatch of straight, straw-colored hair and bristling crescent brows. His eyes, smoky-blue as a stormy sea, filled with concern, brightened when he saw that she was recovering. He smiled down at her. An embarrassed flush stained her cheeks. Huskily she asked, "Who are you?"

"I'm Dan, Dan Kendall." He regarded her with a kind, searching gaze. "More to the point, who are *you*, and are you all right?"

Ashly smiled, but when she spoke, her voice shook.

"I'm Ashly Swann, and—and I'm right as rain."

How could she tell this strange man that she'd had a nightmare and the panic button had been pushed again? Always, before the crash, she'd coped with every crisis, handled every problem. She'd thought herself blessed with more courage and determination than most people. But now, all the courage and determination in the world didn't count.

A flood of despair surged through her. All she wanted was to regain control of her life. To conquer this new and terrible paralyzing fear that squeezed her heart. To fly again for Palm Air. To know once more the sense of freedom and exhilaration that flying always gave her. She wished she hadn't let Jessamine and Ted talk her into staying on with them. But they had convinced her that she needed to be with them until she had gotten over these infernal nightmares and flashbacks. True, they came further and further apart, but would they never end?

Forcing a smile, Ashly started to sit up, but Dan pressed her head snugly back in the curve of his shoulder.

"Take it easy—you still look a little rocky."

As he gazed down at her, his breath warm on her cheek, her heartbeat quickened. She was intensely aware of him: the comforting feel of his strong arms holding her close; his springy chest hair brushing her skin; the salt-sea scent of his body pressed against hers. All lent a false intimacy to the encounter. A small wave of panic fluttered inside her. Quickly, she slid from his arms onto the sand and sat with her knees drawn up to her chin, her arms wrapped around them. In a faint, breathless voice, she said, "I'm fine, really. Just fine."

His quick look of relief changed to one of puzzlement.

"What happened out there? Did you surface too fast?"

At once her face went blank as though a cloud had passed over obscuring her features. "It's—it's just something that happens now and then."

In kind, compassionate tones, he asked, "Want to tell me about it?"

Ashly's throat tightened, her face took on a closed look. She lowered her gaze, staring down at her toes curled in the sand. She had never told anyone what had really happened. To her own surprise, she found she wanted to tell this kind, soft-spoken stranger—who, oddly, made her feel she'd known him all her life. Why it seemed easier to tell a stranger secrets of her heart than to tell someone she loved, she couldn't fathom. She took a deep breath.

"Well, you see, there are these nightmares, and sometimes I panic." She paused, waiting to see his reaction. His expression was warm, caring, interested. He said nothing, but sat still and silent, watching her, not asking questions, nor prying, nor giving advice.

"I can't help it. It just happens—" She wanted to go on, but as always the words stuck in her throat. She couldn't bring herself to talk about what happened—to this gentle stranger, to Jessamine or Ted, to her trauma counselor, anyone. She had locked it away in a dark corner of her mind. That way, she could live with it.

Dan's lips curved in an encouraging smile. "Maybe I can help. I'm a great listener."

An unwelcome feeling of helplessness overtook her. "I've tried everything I know, and everything everyone else knows."

"A therapist?"

"Been there, done that. There's nothing more I can do. I'm afraid time is the only cure." She suppressed a sigh. *"Time* can mean an eternity. I found that out. Just when I begin to relax, another one sneaks up and clobbers me."

He reached out, imprisoned both her hands in his and gazed deeply into her eyes. "I want to help you, believe me."

Her heart gave a painful lurch. He was so earnest, so eager to help, that hope flared when she knew there was none.

"I've told myself a thousand times, if I stop thinking about them, they'll go away. I'm counting on it."

Withdrawing her hands from his, she began combing her fingers though her drenched hair. "It does no good to talk about them."

His mouth curved in an amiable grin. "Okay, change of subject. Do you have any idea how far out you'd drifted? Way beyond your depth? Thank God I saw you floundering around out there."

Ashly smiled. "I'm really an expert swimmer."

He gave a doubtful shake of his head. "You could have fooled me! I thought you were in trouble, jumping up and down in a panic, struggling to keep your head above water."

Ashly laughed up at him. An embarrassed flush crept up her face into her hairline. "Actually, I was frolicking with the porpoises."

A relieved expression shone in his eyes. "That I can believe. I've enjoyed a few frolics with the porpoises myself." He grinned down at her, revealing glistening white teeth and laugh lines carved at the corners of his wide, full lips. His appreciative gaze strayed from the top of her head to her toes.

Under his admiring glance she became aware of her hair straggling like seaweed over her shoulders, the windbreaker fallen open, her gown plastered to her body revealing every curve of breast and thigh. She must look like a wraith cast up from the sea.

An amused glint lighted his eyes and he extended his hands palms up in an appealing gesture. "And I thought I'd saved your life!"

Ashly laughed, and thought how good it felt to laugh again. "I doubt a robot could drown in that sea of salt."

His expression turned solemn. "Actually, saving people and animals from themselves and each other seems to be my lot in life."

Impulsively she reached out to clasp his hand in hers and allow him to draw her to her feet. "Well then, thanks. Thanks for coming to my rescue."

"Any time," he replied solemnly. "Day or night." His fingers closed warmly around hers and somehow she found the gesture reassuring.

"Now tell me what you do when you're not saving lives."

A spark of enthusiasm lighted his eyes and his lips curved in a disarming smile. "Oh, I guess you could say I'm the resident beachcomber. The city fathers keep me here for local color." He cocked his head to one side. "And you?"

Ashly withdrew her hands from his and looked away. She didn't want to be rude, but telling him about herself would only encourage him. And that would be unfair. She would have to make clear that their acquaintance could go no further. Softly she said, "I'm a tourist. Just passing through."

She thought she saw a glimmer of disappointment flicker in his eyes then vanish.

"When may I see you again?"

Ashly felt the muscles in the back of her neck tense, all her defenses alert to danger. Again she looked away, avoiding his hopeful gaze. "I'm sorry. I'm afraid that's impossible."

"Impossible?" One bristly blond eyebrow rose in surprise. He eyed the fingers of her left hand. "Husband?"

She hesitated for a long moment, considering. If she told him she was a widow, would he ask when, and what had caused Werner's death? Dan looked like the kind of man who would offer her sympathy and understanding. A sympathy she couldn't endure. She would be acting a lie. And if she told him so, wouldn't he think her callous? Of course he would, unless she explained about her life with Werner. She gave a vigorous shake of her head. "No husband."

"Well, why then? Why can't I see you?"

"Can't, that's all."

The corners of his mouth quirked in an appealing grin. "Lady, when a beachcomber finds a treasure on the beach, it's finders keepers. I won't take no for an answer!"

Gently she said, "It's the way it is." She shrugged off his windbreaker and thrust it into his hands. "Thanks so much, and goodbye, Dan Kendall." She spun away from him and with quick, light steps fled across the pale, powdery sands, the wind whipping her hair. She dared not look back, but she could feel his eyes following her as she sped down the beach toward Jessamine's cottage.

Chapter 2

"Good heavens, Ashly, what on earth happened to you?

Jessamine's worried exclamation brought Ashly up short in the doorway. Her gaze swept the screened patio past a jungle of tropical plants to the white wrought iron table set for three where Jessamine and Ted were lingering over toast and coffee.

Jessamine, wearing a gentian blue caftan that matched her eyes, and her glossy black hair drawn back from her high rounded forehead, appeared as elegant and graceful as the high-fashion model she had once been. Now, clearly reassured that Ashly was alive and unharmed, her anxious expression vanished, replaced by joy and relief. She rose from the table, crossed to Ashly's side and kissed her lightly on the cheek. "You're just in time for breakfast, love."

Ted's usually affable features were distorted by a frown of mingled bafflement and concern. Still, Ashly noted, he'd shaved, brushed his shining brown hair neatly to one side, and donned kelly green slacks and a yellow sport shirt that complemented his tall, spindly frame. Ashly smiled inwardly. Ted was always ready for anything . He welcomed each day like a man jumping on a merry-go-round, hand outstretched to grab the brass ring. But she couldn't fault him, for his go-for-it attitude had made him a super salesman for Sundance Resorts.

He regarded Ashly from soft gray eyes that on occasion could turn sharp as a finely honed steel blade. His normally warm, Southern drawl held a gentle reproach. "We've been worried about you, Ashly, honey. Where've you been? And in your nightie too."

Ashly was silent for a moment, not wanting to upset Jessamine and Ted further by telling them the real reason she'd fled from the house. Worse, Jessamine might decide to cancel her Newcomers meeting today. It wasn't till now, two months after the crash, that Ashly had been able to persuade Jessamine to leave her here alone. Afraid Ashly would have an anxiety attack, or sink into depression, Jessamine had refused invitations, refused to go swimming, refused even to go food shopping without her. Jess was hellbent on looking after her. Ashly's vigorous protests that she didn't need anyone were met with smiles and the implacable resistance of a stone wall.

Hating herself for dissembling, Ashly murmured, "Sorry, I—I woke up early, when it was still dark, and took a stroll—shelling." Grinning, she added, "If I look bedraggled, it's because I went for a swim."

Ted eyed her fondly and gave a rueful shake of his head. "You're one crazy lady, honey, out there shellin' in the dark. We'll sure have to keep a closer watch on you."

Though his tone was jovial, Ashly knew he meant it. Meant to make her feel cared for, less alone in the world. And meant to keep her from hurting herself if she couldn't handle all the anger and guilt and depression that continued to plague her after the crash. A small flash of annoyance, almost rebellion flared inside her. Instantly she felt ashamed. She should be grateful that her sister and brother-in-law cared so deeply about her. Why wasn't she more appreciative?

Before she could sort out her thoughts, she saw Jessamine glance quickly at the corner shelf where the long shelling sticks and flashlights used for pre-dawn shelling expeditions were still in place. Jessamine's gaze flicked back to Ashly in mute understanding.

Ashly blushed, embarrassed at being caught in her deception. Jessamine knew. Knew she hadn't gone shelling. Had she guessed that another nightmare had driven her from the house? In low, compassionate tones, Jessamine said, "You look chilled to the bone, darling. Better change into dry clothes while I scramble a few eggs."

Glad to escape further questioning, Ashly retreated to her room. Once under the shower, she luxuriated in the warm water coursing down her slender body, lathering with rose-scented soap, rinsing the sticky salt and sand from her skin and hair. After a rubdown with a fluffy white towel, she brushed her hair to a bright golden sheen, flung on a teal blue sleeveless top, tomato-red skirt, burlap belt, and espadrilles, and hurried back to the lanai.

As she slid into a chair at the table, Ted glanced at her inquiringly. "Find any neat shells this morning?"

Ashly felt hot color creep up her face into her hairline. "Nothing unusual. Nine million clam shells." Why didn't she tell him? She had nothing to hide, for heaven's sake. She stabbed her fork into a mound of scrambled eggs Jessamine set before her.

Ted leaned back in his chair and gazed at Ashly over the rim of his coffee cup.

"Thought I saw you visiting with some fella on the beach."

Ashly felt his warm, curious gaze upon her. Had he seen her talking with Dan Kendall, or nestled in the shelter of Dan's arms under the blue and white cabana? For a reason she couldn't explain, she didn't want to share her encounter with the charming stranger on the beach. She wanted to cherish those private moments, when for a short while a stranger had made her feel admired and desired. Lowering her gaze, she spread kumquat jam slowly and carefully on a slice of toast.

"Oh?"

Ted persisted pleasantly. "Anyone we know?"

Ted was just curious, Ashly told herself. Just looking after her. Not accusing her of anything. Over a bit of toast that had lodged in her throat, she murmured, "Probably not."

Jessamine turned an indulgent smile on her husband. "Ted is determined to meet every soul on Sanibel Island! He's never met a stranger."

"Best not to take up with strangers," Ted warned. "Even paradise has a few bad apples."

"He picked me up off the beach like a seashell," said Ashly cheerfully, and at once regretted her unfortunate choice of words.

"Does he have a name?" asked Ted, smiling.

"Ken . . . somebody Kendall, I think he said. . . ." She let her voice trail off.

Ted's smile vanished as he and Jessamine exchanged startled glances.

"Would that be Dan Kendall?" Jessamine asked.

"No doubt!" Ted snapped, his lips set in a disapproving frown. He took a sip of coffee as if to dispel an unpleasant taste in his mouth.

Ashly regarded him in mild surprise. "Then you know him?"

"As well as we care to." Ted set his cup down hard on the saucer. "He's nothing but a beach bum. Spends half his life roaming the beach, bucketing around in a battered MG. A no-account good-for-nothing! Never seen him do an honest day's work. Just makes himself available for squirin' wealthy women around the island. Know what I mean?"

Ashly felt a small stab of disappointment. That hadn't been her impression of Dan Kendall.

Defensively, she asked, "How do you know this? After all, you and Jess have only lived here six months."

Irritably, Ted went on. "I've been told that last year, every time Sundance Resorts applied for a new building permit, he'd raise cain about preserving the island ecology.

The man's an agitator, a real troublemaker. I'd steer clear of him, Ashly, honey."

Unaccountably annoyed by Ted's criticism of the stranger who'd tried to "save her life," Ashly said nothing, but assumed a bland expression, glad he couldn't know what she was thinking: *If you were me, you'd seek him out, and run straight into his strong, sheltering arms.*

Recalling the ecstatic moments when Dan Kendall had held her close in his comforting embrace, her heart warmed. The man was an original, like no one she'd ever met either in the sheltered New England village of her childhood, in conservative Boston, or in glittering, cosmopolitan Washington, D.C. She found him utterly intriguing. But a relationship with any man now was unthinkable.

Jessamine poured coffee into Ashly's cup. "Ted, I think you're judging the man unfairly. Ashly's right. We haven't lived here long enough to really know him. You're just ticked off because he opposed Sundance building condos."

Ted's brows rose in mock indignation. "All I'm doin' is protectin' my women like we Southern boys always do."

"I don't plan to see him again," said Ashly quietly.

"Of course not, dear," agreed Jessamine in sympathetic tones. She glanced at the clock, then at Ted. "Newcomers meets in exactly half an hour. I've got to rush. Why don't you drop me on your way to work? Ashly can have the VW and I'll catch a ride home with someone."

Smiling, Ted folded his hands behind his head and leaning back in his chair, stretched his long legs out before him. "I'm not fixin' to fight my way through the jungle this early in the morning. No one buys condos before ten A.M. Take the VW, Jess. I'll drive Ashly anywhere she wants to go. No harm in takin' a little time out from work."

"No, please!" Ashly protested. *Here they go again,* she thought, *going out of their way for me.* She hated to foul up their routine. She knew they worried that she would have an anxiety attack or fly off the handle, really lose it and have an accident, but they were too polite to say so. "Don't worry about me," she said firmly. "I'm not going anywhere."

"Whatever you say, love!" Jessamine rose from the table, dropped a light kiss atop Ashly's smooth, golden hair and left.

Ted poured another cup of coffee for each of them, propped his elbows on the table and leaned toward Ashly. Ashly saw in his eyes a gleam of brotherly interest and devotion that forewarned her of confidences about to be shared. She felt suddenly uneasy.

"You know, I have to hand it to Jessamine. She's been a good sport, going along with Sundance moving me to Florida. I was afraid, Yankee that she is, she'd hate living on an island off the coast. But I'd say she's taken to life here, wouldn't you?"

Ashly studied him for a moment without speaking. Did Ted honestly believe Jessamine was happy here? she wondered. True, Jessamine, gave the appearance of being happy, but when Ashly arrived in Sanibel six weeks ago, she was immediately aware of Jessamine's distraught manner, her pensive silences. At first she'd thought Jessamine's moods were a reaction to her own brush with death. Jess had rushed to Ashly's side in the hospital; arranged Werner's funeral, closed up their house. But as weeks passed, Jessamine's abstracted air remained and there was an unrest about her, a tenseness that signaled trouble. Plainly, there was something bothering her other than Ashly's plight.

Months ago, Jessamine had pleaded with Ashly to visit her, claimed she was dying of loneliness. Werner had protested then, and Ashly had given in. A wave of remorse swept through her. If only she hadn't let Werner talk her out of going when Jessamine first urged her to visit, maybe she could have helped. All their lives they had shared their triumphs and failures, their happiness and sorrows. Now that Jessamine was married to Ted, she kept her own counsel, and Ashly refused to pry into her sister's private life.

DREAM OF LOVE 21

Jessamine would confide in her when she was ready, and as always, Ashly would be there for her.

She had no doubt Jessamine still loved Ted. He was one of those men who adore women. And women adored him. He had certainly bowled Jessamine off her feet. It wasn't hard to impress a starry-eyed nineteen-year-old. For three lean years after their parents' death in a car crash, Ashly had supported Jessamine and herself and insisted she could see Jessamine through college. But Jessamine had protested that Ashly had struggled long enough. It was time to strike out on her own. Against Ashly's wishes, Jessamine, lured by the glamour and excitement of New York had left Boston U. in her sophomore year for a modeling career. In New York, she'd met Ted LeBeau, a Florida transplant and manufacturer's rep for Seventh Avenue Couturier Fashions. Handsome, sophisticated, silver-tongued, Ted had courted her with flair. Wine and roses, candy and perfume, intimate candlelit dinners, theater, concerts. What woman could resist such flattering attention? Certainly not Jessamine, thought Ashly wryly.

Ashly had been as thrilled and happy as Jessamine when he'd proposed, thankful that her sister had a chance for happiness. When the newlyweds pleaded with Ashly to live with them in their apartment in an elegant brownstone, Ashly smiled, shaking her head. "No way! For the first time in my life I'll be living alone and I'm going to love it!" She had rejoiced in her total independence, until she'd met Werner Hoffman.

Now she became aware of Ted's expectant gaze boring in on her as he waited for her reply. Ashly nodded. "Surprising, when you consider what an exciting and fascinating life Jessamine led in New York."

Ted scowled, stirred his coffee. "Maybe I shouldn't have uprooted her. But when this opening with Sundance Resorts came along—anyway, at the time, Jess seemed thrilled to be moving here...." his voice trailed off.

Instantly Ashly wondered if he was fishing to see what she knew. Ashly grinned. "Sanibel's a great place. And

Jessamine's always hated cold weather. To her, hell is a winter in Boston. Besides, you're her whole life. And she'd never stand in the way of her man—a man on his way up."

Ted's gray eyes brightened. "You bet I was on my way up. This was a once-in-a-lifetime chance to get in on the ground floor with a dynamite company." His face glowed with pride and enthusiasm. "Do you realize that in less than five years Sundance has built resort condos in Vail, Hawaii, the Costa del Sol, and Athens?"

Ashly's clear blue eyes sparkled with amusement. "I suspected you were doing well when you bought Jessamine kruggerands to wear in her penny loafers."

Ted laughed. "It was my way of tellin' her we were movin' on. And this is only the beginnin'!" He rubbed his palms together in an exultant gesture. "We're going to build in Naples, Boca Grande, and Captiva, as well as Sanibel, and your little sister Jessamine, my precious jewel, will be placed in the settin' she deserves. She'll never regret givin' up modelin'!"

Ashly stared down at the table, avoiding his gaze. She wasn't so sure about that. Ted always assumed everyone else thought exactly as he did—and he thought Jessamine had it all. But Ted meant well, she told herself. He always meant well.

As though struck by a thought, Ted went on. "I imagine you found life in Washington pretty exciting after Boston."

Ashly shook her head. "Please, let's not talk about Washington, or Boston." But he'd jogged her memory and scenes flashed through her mind like color slides on a screen: her graduation day at Palm Air Academy; Jessamine, a picture-book bride; Ashly's wedding in the parlor of a justice of the peace, after a one-month, whirlwind courtship.

They'd met on a flight to Washington, D.C., where Werner was a lobbyist for a chemical company. She had been captivated by Werner's forceful personality, impressed by his polished veneer, his *savoir faire*, his air of strength and stability; dazzled by the glamorous life he offered her in the nation's capital. He seemed all she could desire in a husband. Married less than a year, thought Ashly dispiritedly, it seemed a lifetime—and for Werner, it was. She closed her mind against further painful memories of her marriage to Werner.

In determined, no-nonsense tones, she said, "Ted, I know you're only staying home to keep me company, and it isn't necessary, really. I won't be lonely."

How could she tell him she was longing for a day of her own—a luxury she'd not known in her entire married life? On days she wasn't flying for Palm Air, Werner had never wanted her out of his sight. And now Jessamine and Ted were shepherding her around like a lost lamb.

Ted reached across the table and took Ashly's hand in his warm clasp. "You don't ever need to feel lonely. Jess and I will always look after you."

Gently withdrawing her hand from his, she started to say that it wasn't looking after she needed, but time alone, time to figure out why she had been spared when so many people had died in the crash. Time to work through the guilt. Instead, she jumped up from the table and swept silver and plates onto a tray. "Go on to work, Ted. I'll clean up the kitchen."

Ted stood up, looking relieved and slightly apologetic. "I do have a stack of paperwork waitin'—if you're sure you'll be all right here by yourself. . . ."

Ashly flashed him a reassuring smile. "Absolutely."

Ted raised a hand in mock salute and left.

Thoughtfully, Ashly loaded plates into the dishwasher. Ted seemed to think Jessamine was happy here. Had he brought up the subject because he was looking for reassurance from her? A slight frown creased her brow. If Jess really was happy here, why her pensive silences and abstracted air? Ashly caught her lower lip between her teeth. She would watch, and wait.

Chapter 3

With a small sigh of pleasure Ashly stood up and surveyed the flower beds she had finished weeding. Satisfied that the scarlet geraniums and white and purple petunias looked as neat as she could make them, she glanced at her watch. Only ten-thirty. Her heart lifted in anticipation. She had the rest of the morning free to spend as she pleased.

She carried the bamboo broom, rake, and black plastic sack filled with weeds to the garage and stashed them away in a corner. There, a green three-speed bike caught her eye. Impulsively, she climbed onto the seat. Her feet bore down on the pedals and the next moment she was coasting down the driveway. A heady sense of freedom gave her wings. She swung left and streaked along the narrow blacktop road.

Breathless, exhilarated, she rolled past fields studded with squat palmettos and high, thick bushes sprouting scarlet berries. On her left rose gleaming white, cubelike buildings set among green lawns, swaying palms, tennis courts, and a sparkling turquoise pool. One of Ted's Sundance Resorts, thought Ashly impressed. Another monument to his success. The man could sell mink coats to a nudist colony.

She let out a frustrated sigh. If only her own life were set on course. Right now she felt like a passenger on an unscheduled flight, doomed to circle forever in a holding pattern waiting for clearance to land. Her counselor had warned her that it wouldn't be easy. Palm Air had given her medical leave to go through therapy and until she was well, they would not permit her to fly again. But therapy had not stopped the flashbacks, the anxiety attacks. With desperate resolve, she clenched her jaw, tightened her grip on the handlebars and sped on.

As she pedaled past a shady woodland of feathery Australian pines and sabal palms, a sudden gleam of sunshine bathed the scene in a golden light, warming the top of her head, her back, her arms. A sense of euphoria spread through her, filling her with optimism.

She slowed at a break in the trees, her attention caught by a neat redwood sign: SANIBEL ISLAND NATURE CENTER, VISITORS WELCOME. She skidded to a stop, slid her bike into an iron rack then strolled up a crushed shell path to a low, rustic-looking building of gray stone, glass and wood. Inside the bright, spacious lobby, she was drawn toward lighted glass cases mounted on the walls. Fascinated, she gazed at displays of shells, photographs of trees and plants and various species of wildlife—birds, raccoons, alligators—living on the island. Here was a strange and exciting world—one she knew nothing about.

She glanced briefly at the display in the gift shop and crossed to the information desk. Behind it sat a short, plump woman with a halo of gray hair, lively brown eyes and a dimpled smile. She wore a red skirt and a red-and-white checked shirt with a name tag that read Martha Kirby.

"Would you like to buy a ticket for the nature walk? It starts in just five minutes."

Ashly gave a regretful shake of her head. "Love to, but I rushed off without my billfold."

The woman's smile widened. "You look honest. You can drop the money off later." She nodded toward a cluster of people who stood chatting before double glass doors at the far end of the lobby. "You're welcome to join the tour."

Smiling her thanks, Ashly crossed to the group of visitors and stood staring through the glass doors at the lush green woodland beyond. She started at the sound of a warm, resonant voice behind her.

"I've been involved with the Nature Center since its beginning ten years ago, and will be your guide this morning. Please don't hesitate to ask questions during our walk."

Ashly spun around and stood staring into Dan Kendall's cobalt-blue eyes. His intense gaze held hers and one bristly blond brow rose in surprise. Unaccountably, her heartbeat quickened. She couldn't tear her gaze from his. Standing there in the sunlight, wearing faded jeans and blue denim shirt open at the throat, binoculars slung on a strap around his neck, he had the cheerful, relaxed air of a man accustomed to meeting life on his own terms and coming out the victor. It struck her then that though he wasn't the handsomest man she'd ever met, he was surely the most virile and the most earthly.

Pleased recognition glistened in his eyes and the corners of his mouth quirked in a conspiratorial grin, as if to share an inside joke. "How's the newest member of the porpoise family this morning?"

Ashly grinned back and matched his bantering tone. "I'm fine, the family's fine...." Suddenly cautious, she thought better of it and let her voice trail off. It would be a mistake to encourage him—not because Ted had warned her against him, but because the last thing she needed was an emotional entanglement to complicate her life. Romance was not on her agenda.

Dan stepped forward and standing only a breath away, gazed down at her. His amused expression gave way to concern as his eyes searched hers, probing their depths so intently that Ashly felt he could read the innermost secrets of her soul.

"Seriously, everything cool with you now?"

"Chilled," she replied with a shade too much conviction.

Dan cocked his head and his lips curved in a boyish, disarming grin that made her knees weak. "I'm glad you decided to look me up."

Unnerved by his smiling self-assurance, she said in quick denial, "Oh, but I didn't. I'm here for the nature walk."

Pinpoints of light, like secret laughter sparkled in his eyes. Clearly he didn't believe her. But all he said was, "And I'll be your guide today. So let's move on out!"

As he reached around her to push open the heavy glass door, his forearm grazed her shoulder. She jumped and her heart skipped a beat. She felt his eyes on her, questioning her startled reaction. The man missed nothing. She looked away, as if his touch had caused her no more concern than a fly brushing the tip of her nose. He turned toward a large wooden nesting box mounted on the wall and peered inside. "Visiting barn owl," he murmured over his shoulder. "We're hoping she'll nest here, but so far she's just circling around."

When everyone had strolled through the doorway onto a wide boardwalk, Dan began talking about the island in warm, enthusiastic tones.

"Sanibel-Captiva is divided into three sections: beaches, shell ridges, and wetlands—the last supporting the mangroves. The mangroves, on the Pine Island Sound side, are a vitally important resource on the island, for there is where life begins. They provide a food source for invertebrates and fish, and a nesting area for birds as well."

As he went on, it seemed to Ashly that he was speaking solely to her, that his gaze sought her out. Again she turned her head away, afraid he'd read in her eyes more than she wanted him to see. She tried not to listen to this intriguing man who disturbed her thoughts and senses without even trying. But soon she was swept up again, entranced by his low voice as he went on recounting the history of the islands.

"Years ago, the only access to Sanibel was by ferry. Then in sixty-three, the causeway was opened, now the only roadway linking Sanibel to the mainland. People flocked here to live—," abruptly his voice hardened, "—and to ravish the island. We had already established a wildlife sanctuary, and in sixty-seven we passed a land use plan to protect the environment of Sanibel and its sister island Captiva. Each year more than half a million visitors enjoy viewing our refuge lands and wildlife."

His tone was so compelling, his enthusiasm so contagious, that Ashly found herself hanging on every word.

"The entire ecological system of the islands is based on the freshwater system in the interior of Sanibel. The dominant feature, of course, is the Sanibel River." He led the group to the side of the boardwalk and leaning against the railing, nodded toward a dark brackish swamp of saw grass and cattails.

"This marsh is a part of the freshwater wetlands surrounding the river. All of these vast marshes are teeming with wildlife: birds, otters, raccoons, alligators, and fish." He flung out an arm in a sweeping gesture, taking in an expanse of tall, slender grasses. "We call this the 'River of Grass.' It's cord grass, essential to the ecology of the island. Everything breeds here—safe because it's impossible for predators—," his lips curved in a rueful grin, "—animal or human, to penetrate it."

Ashly leaned over the railing and reached toward the furry-looking grasses. At the same instant, a hand shot past her shoulder and strong fingers gripped her wrist, jerking her hand back. She cried out, wrenched free from the viselike grip and spun to face her captor.

Dan stared down at her, his face mirroring mingled alarm and concern. Sharply, he warned, "Don't pick the vegetation!"

Frowning, Ashly rubbed her wrist. Her skin burned with

the imprint of his strong, tanned fingers. "I only wanted to touch it. It looks so soft and feathery."

Dan shook his head. "It *looks* soft, but isn't. If you slide your hand up the blade, it can give you a nasty cut."

He reached out, took her hand in his, and with gentle fingers explored the contours of her slender wrist. "No broken bones, luckily." Grinning down at her, he made a courtly bow, bent his head, kissed the back of her hand, then swung away down a wide dirt path into the woodland.

His romantic behavior threw her off-balance. The man was an enigma. Who was the real Dan Kendall? The man who had dashed into the water to save her and had shown such tenderness and concern for her safety, or the good-natured, easy-going beachcomber who appeared totally irresponsible, without a care in the world—or the intelligent ecologist, volunteer guide and lecturer? The question inflamed her curiosity. She wanted to know more, to know what moved the heart and mind behind the many faces of this compelling stranger, to know the real Dan Kendall.

Covertly she studied his weathered, rough-hewn features: straight nose, strong chin, wide, full-lipped mouth. Her feminine intuition warned her that Dan Kendall might be dangerous to an unwary female.

As the morning wore on, Dan displayed an impressive competence and store of knowledge of the natural world around him. Why, the man's a *flora* and *fauna* freak, thought Ashly, dismayed. Clearly he loved the world of nature and loved talking about it. Listening to him now, his low, vibrant tones struck a responsive chord deep within her.

"And if we wish to continue to enjoy nature's gifts, they must be safeguarded." He turned to survey the group of visitors trailing after him, bestowing on them a warm, infectious grin. "I am one of the guardians."

Dan strode on, his tousled blond head rising above those of the tour group. Ashly, watching the way his broad shoulders swung in rhythm with his step; the way he moved with the supple grace of a jungle animal; the way his sun-streaked hair curled on the nape of his neck, suddenly felt an intense desire to feel his arms around her once again.

Eagerly the tour group followed in Dan's footsteps over shell ridges and low swales; now under the warmth of brilliant sunlight, now in the cool shade of soaring cabbage palms whose trunks had been stripped by marauding raccoons.

Along the wide, shady path he pointed out bayberry bushes whose blue-gray berries were used for making candles, then halted before a spiny shrub with small white berries. Picking one from a cluster of leaves, he split it open with a thumbnail. The berry oozed dark blue liquid. "The Caloosa Indians who lived here four hundred years ago made dye from these berries we call indigo!"

As they ambled on down the winding trail, Dan pointed out the long, dark green, leathery-leaved strangler fig, prickly pear cactus, wild lime, flowering lantana, and fernlike dog fennel, Ashly paused before a high, bushy shrub with red berries. "This is beautiful, what is it?"

Dan gave a disparaging shake of his head. "Brazilian pepper, or Florida holly, scourge of the island and number one pest. It was introduced here years ago by a botanist—possibly to hold the soil—today fifty to seventy percent of the island flora is overrun with it. It deprives our native plants of water and light and room to grow." Dan's lips curved downward in a rueful grin. "Birds love it. They devour the berries, then fly off in loopy spirals in a drunken stupor, dropping seeds everywhere. We're doing our best to eliminate it. We've chopped it down, burned it, but it invades again. Now we're bulldozing certain areas."

Thinking of Ted and Sundance Resorts, Ashly put in eagerly, "Wouldn't the best solution be for a developer to build condos over it?"

Dan's blond brows furrowed in a scowl. In tones of exaggerated patience, he said, "We're trying to *preserve* the island so it will remain a place where people and nature can coexist with joy and benefit to both. You can scarcely exist with Brazilian pepper, and even less with condominiums. There are too many already on Sanibel and Captiva."

Others of the group glared at her reprovingly. Ashly wished she could dive down a rabbit hole. Obviously she'd struck a raw nerve. The man was an ecology freak. There was no reason to take his words personally. Anyway, what did it matter? She'd never see him again.

Rounding a bend in the trail they came upon a weathered wooden observation tower and trooped up the stairs to a platform which offered an excellent view of the coffee-colored waters of the Sanibel River. Dan crossed to Ashly's side and stood focusing his binoculars on a patch of sunlight on the riverbank, while she gazed enraptured at the peaceful scene before her.

Without preamble, Dan handed Ashly the binoculars, looped the leather strap around her neck and curved an arm about her shoulders. "Zero in on that log jutting out from the stand of pepper trees on your right."

Startlingly aware of his body close to hers, his breath warm on her cheek, the earthy, woodsy scent of him, her fingers shook as she adjusted the lenses. As her vision sharpened, she gasped, shrinking back against Dan's broad chest, every nerve ending aflame. "Dan, the log is moving!"

Dan burst out laughing. "Stop shaking. Keep an eye on it."

Ashly bit her lip. Quivering she was, but not because of what she saw through the binoculars. Slowly, the log crept into the water and disappeared into the murky depths.

" 'Gator," said Dan unnecessarily. "They're nocturnal. Won't hurt you unless you go after them."

"No way!" Thrusting the binoculars at Dan, she quickly eased from under his encircling arm. If he thought she was shaking from fear of the alligator, so much the better.

Shortly, to Ashly's relief, Dan led everyone back to the Center where the tour ended. The visitors thanked him for the tour. He thanked them for their interest. Reluctantly, Ashly started to stroll away with the group when she felt a restraining hand on her arm.

"Enjoy the tour?"

Ashly looked around and saw Dan fixing her with a bright, expectant gaze.

"It was fantastic! Like discovering a new world. You're a terrific guide."

He gave her a wry grin. "I should be. For a while I was a perpetual student—got degrees in biology, ecology, you name it. Actually, I'm the director of the Center."

"Director!" exclaimed Ashly, astonished. A flicker of joy kindled inside her. Ted was all wrong about Dan. "I should have known a volunteer guide wouldn't have all your knowledge and enthusiasm."

Dan gave a vigorous shake of his head. "Our volunteers are *all* knowledgeable and enthusiastic. As a matter of fact, I'm a volunteer."

Feeling suddenly deflated, Ashly murmured, "I see." A wave of disappointment swept through her. Perhaps Ted was right after all. Dan didn't work to support himself. Did he exist on the generosity of the wealthy women of Sanibel?

In a voice filled with anticipation, he asked, "When may I see you again?"

She looked up into his face, her clear blue luminous gaze locking with his. "Never," she said firmly.

His crescent brows lifted. "Never is a mighty long time. Believe me, I know. My wife Carol died three years ago. Never to see her, to be with her again, has been tough."

"Oh, I'm sorry...."

He raised a hand as if to cut off any further expression of sympathy.

"Life goes on, whether you like it or not, and I haven't been exactly hibernating. Forced myself to go out, to date other women. But I've never found one who interested me—until I met you."

She didn't intend to sound sharp, but because she had to force words she didn't want to say, they came out hard and cold, dropping like stones. "Sorry. I don't date."

The bright, interested light in his eyes died, replaced by a cool, impersonal glint. "Whatever you say." He turned, strode across the lobby and disappeared down a sunny corridor.

A sinking feeling of dropping too fast in an elevator, surged through her. All she wanted was to get out of here. She bolted toward the door and passing Martha's desk, thanked her for allowing her to take the tour, and hurried out.

Pedaling homeward along the San-Cap Road, her mind churned with thoughts of Dan. The more she thought about him, the more uneasy she became. The trouble was, she wanted to see him again, but common sense told her she must never see him again. Not because Ted disliked him, but because she feared her own responses to him. She found him infinitely fascinating and intriguing. He aroused in her feelings of longing and desire she thought had died, stirred her as no other man ever had. A hot wave of guilt washed through her. How could she feel so drawn to this man when Werner was scarcely cold in his grave? Shame mingled with guilt. She was much too vulnerable, far too responsive to Dan Kendall's warm, gentle touch, the appealing look in his eyes. But he was funny and caring and fun to be with, and he made her forget the tragedy in her life. Somehow, it seemed all the more reason to avoid him.

Chapter 4

The next morning, eager to bask in the sun on the beach, Ashly kept one eye on her watch, counting the minutes till she was sure Dan Kendall would be on duty at the Nature Center. Shortly after ten, wearing a royal blue bikini, she spread her yellow cover-up on the sand, flopped down on her stomach and opened the whodunit she'd brought along to read. She had no idea how long she lay contentedly reading in the warm sunshine when a shadow fell across the page. Shading her eyes with one hand, she looked up. Dan stood gazing down at her with a wide, lopsided grin. He wore a white t-shirt, frayed cut-offs and tattered tennis shoes, tanned toes pushing through the threadbare canvas. She smiled to herself. No doubt the tennies were old friends from whom he couldn't bear to part. The thought was somehow endearing.

Steeling herself against his beguiling smile, she looked down at her book, and forced herself to say the words she knew she should say. "I meant what I said yesterday, about our not meeting again." To her annoyance, her voice was soft and gentle and lacked conviction.

Dan frowned, shaking his head. "Never is too long."

As if he hadn't spoken, she went on, "I won't be here much longer, so there's no point in becoming involved with people on the island."

He sank down on the sand beside her and stretched out his long legs on the sand. "I'm not *people*, there's only one of me. And who said anything about becoming involved?"

Hot color stained her cheeks. She rolled over and sat up, looking him straight in the eyes. "Still, it would be better if we didn't see any more of each other."

A spark of deviltry lighted his eyes as he scooped up a handful of sand and let it sift through his square, tanned fingers. "Better for whom?"

"Better for both of us," she said gently.

He smiled into her eyes. "Wrong! You're entitled to your opinion, of course. And I'm entitled to mine." He leaned back on his elbows and his warm appreciative gaze traveled the length of her trim figure from her pink, polished toenails upward over gently curving hips, lingering on her high, small breasts, coming to rest on her flushed face. "And I happen to disagree with you."

She looked up at him, dumbstruck.

His eyes crinkled at the corners and the mischievous glint in them deepened. Laughter quirked at the corners of his mouth. "Anyway, you have no choice. This is a public beach."

Unaccustomed to people who didn't take her at her word, she felt flustered, confused. With a hopeless shake of her head she jumped to her feet, dashed across the sand, and splashed into the cooling waters of the Gulf.

She dived headlong into the waves. If she disappeared from sight, maybe Dan would go away. She squeezed her eyes shut and held her breath until she thought her lungs would burst. At last she surfaced, shaking her head, dashing salt water from her eyes. Good. He was gone.

A congratulatory voice at her back said, "You swim almost as well as the porpoises!"

Ashly whipped around. Dan floated on his back, watching her, an admiring look in his eyes. He'd shed his shirt, shorts and sneakers, and wore only a red Speedo. Blushing, she stared at his tanned, muscular body thinking, *the man is beautiful!*

Laughter bubbled in her throat. Swiftly, she swung about and headed toward shore, swimming as though a killer shark were after her. She had gained only a few yards when a hand gripping her ankle like a band of steel pulled her backward.

"Let go!" Ashly shrieked, flailing the air in pretended panic.

Dan's laughter echoed in her ears. The next instant his arms went around her and he pulled her to him, hugging her close against his glistening, bronzed chest.

Against her will, Ashly inhaled the fresh, salt-sea smell of him, reveled in the strength of his arms about her. She forced herself to shout, "Dan Kendall, let me go!"

At once he released his bear-hug hold, but the next moment his strong hands gripped her tightly about the waist. He lifted her slender body high over his head. Grinning up into her face he shouted, "Don't struggle. I'm saving your life again!"

Laughing down at him, she took a quick gasp of air, planted her feet on his broad shoulders and pushed off, plunging into the dark, briny waters.

Arms and legs churning, she swam about until she saw Dan's long legs floating above her in the bluish, undulating waves. She swam toward him, grasped his ankles and with all her strength, yanked downward. Taken by surprise, Dan dropped like an anchor. Laughing to herself, Ashly shot to the surface.

Dan bobbed up beside her, his hair plastered to his head, A wicked grin curved his lips as he shook off shimmering droplets of water. He clamped his hands on her shoulders, leaned forward and kissed the tip of her nose. Tiny shock waves tingled through her. Quickly, she slipped from his grasp. With her open palm she struck the water and sent a sparkling plume flying toward him. A comical, astonished expression came over his face. Ashly burst out laughing.

With mock outrage, he lunged toward her. Giggling, she fell backward and with a strong backstroke eluded his outstretched arms. With porpoiselike grace, she rolled over and stroked downward toward the sandy floor of the Gulf. Moments later she surfaced several yards from her indignant pursuer.

He fixed her with a steely-eyed glare, then swiftly submerged and plowed wildly through the water after her. She raced from the water and flopped down on the beach, breathless and laughing from the pleasure and excitement of their chase.

Dan dropped down beside her, grinning, shaking his head. "You're the prettiest porpoise I've ever seen. What do you do in real life—synchronized swimming?"

She hesitated and avoiding his gaze looked down at her feet. "At the moment . . . nothing much. I used to be a flight attendant."

"Why did you quit?"

"I—I got burned out," she said flatly. "End of story." She smiled up at him then, her eyes glowing with pleasure. "Swimming with the porpoises is super. I haven't had so much fun in years!" Startled, she realized it was true.

"Nor have I," he said softly. His deep blue eyes, filled with longing, locked with hers.

Uncomfortable with the warm intimacy of his gaze, she said, "Don't you have to show up at the Center this morning?"

He glanced down at his watch. "Good Lord, yes. I'm late." He swept up his t-shirt, shorts, and tennies and smiled into her eyes. "See you tomorrow, same time, same place." Without waiting for her reply, he gave her a jaunty salute and left.

With his leaving, the sunlight seemed to fade from the day. It upset her to realize how much she had enjoyed being with him. "Tomorrow," he'd said, "same time, same place." Did she dare meet him again? Surely there could be no harm in whiling away a few pleasant hours on the beach, she thought wistfully, in view of the entire world.

It wasn't the same as a date. She would see him only in passing. Dreamily she replayed in her mind every happy moment of the hours she had spent with Dan Kendall. A small stab of guilt ran through her.

That night he invaded her dreams, smiling, laughing into her eyes, his large, strong hands gripping her shoulders, her narrow waist, his powerful arms pulling her to him, holding her tightly, so that she ached with longing for him. By the time morning came, in the clear, bright light of day, Ashly knew what harm there could be in basking on the beach with Dan Kendall. It wasn't that she couldn't rely on him to take her at her word; she couldn't rely on herself. Widowed and lonely, she was enjoying his company far too much to trust her own wayward heart. Though it pained her to do it, she would have to banish him from her life. She told herself, again and again, that in the long run, it was for the best.

To make certain to avoid him, she arose before breakfast, donned her royal blue bikini and let herself out of the cottage quietly so as not to awaken Jessamine and Ted. Spreading her yellow cover-up on the beach, she sat down and opened her book. For awhile she was distracted by shellers strolling along the water's edge, but soon became engrossed in reading. Gradually the disquieting feeling came over her that she was being watched. Startled, she glanced up from her book. Dan, hands on his hips, head cocked to one side, stood watching her, an eager expression shining from his eyes.

Ashly couldn't disguise her pleasure. "Oh, it's you!"

His smiling gaze caressed her lithe, tanned figure. "You're early! Were you expecting someone else?" His eyes probed hers, questioning.

Her breath caught in her throat. "No, no one else." In no-nonsense tones meant to send him on his way, she said, "Nor did I expect you."

DREAM OF LOVE

"You disappoint me. I thought you were here early because you couldn't wait to see me."

Sternly she reminded herself that she wanted no further involvement with this beguiling man. She took a deep breath, racking her mind for the right words to convince him to leave her alone. Instead, she asked brightly, "Where are you off to, so early in the morning?"

"I was on my way to the lighthouse to check out a few things till it was time to meet you." But he stood unmoving, a cheerful grin on his face, watching her.

Reluctantly she rose to her feet. Once again she tried to make herself say the words to send him away, out of her life.

"Well," she faltered, "don't let me keep you. I—I'm going shelling." She flung her cover-up around her shoulders and walked with brisk, resolute steps across the soft white sand, away from the direction of the lighthouse.

Dan fell into step beside her, matching her stride. "There's nothing I like more than early-morning shelling."

"I—I'd rather go alone."

He gave a vigorous shake of his head. "Better not. A stranger might accost you on the beach and . . ."

An impish smile lighted Ashly's eyes. "You accosted me on the beach. I didn't know you from Adam."

He quirked an eyebrow in reproof. "I saved your life. That's different."

Laughing, Ashly turned to face him. "You did *not* save my life!"

Grinning, Dan said, "I prefer to think I did. Justifies my existence."

Nonplussed, Ashly shook her head. "How can I deny a man his right to exist?"

"Besides," he went on in his slow, resonant drawl, "I'm going your way."

Astonished, Ashly said, "You said you were going to the lighthouse."

With good-humored cheer, he replied, "I changed my mind."

She smiled to herself. The man was impossible. "Right! And I've changed *my* mind." In no-nonsense tones she went on, "I can't see you today, or any other day." She swung away from him and head high, struck out down the beach. Broken shells cut into her toes, so that she had to slow down to watch her steps. Head bent, she continued down the beach. She started at the sound of a warm, friendly voice over her shoulder.

"Watch it! You'll get the Sanibel Stoop! It's one of the hazards of shelling."

She turned her head and smiled in spite of herself. Dan, bent almost double, head down in a comical pose, was scanning the shining wet sand for seashells.

"I'll risk it!" said Ashly, strolling on ahead.

He straightened, and with quick strides caught up with her. "Sanibel has some of the best shelling beaches in the world!"

Ashly made no reply, wishing that he would simply go away.

Dan ambled at her side, stooping now and then to pick up a shell. Unperturbed, apparently unaware of her resolute silence, he rattled on, naming the shells, sharing with her the beauty of their delicate coloring and exquisite design and describing the sea creatures they housed.

"Ah!" he exclaimed, elated. "Here's one you don't often find." He picked up an elongated oval-shaped, brown-spotted shell. "A junonia." He held the gleaming shell on his open palm. "For you!" Solemnly, he took her hand in his and placed it reverently in her palm, as though bestowing a gift on a queen.

Her heart turned over. How could she refuse the gift of a shell? "Thank you." She curled her fingers about the smooth, oval junonia and thrust her hand deep in the pocket of her cover-up. His gift of the rare and lovely shell meant nothing, she assured herself. It was a gesture of friendship, that's all. Friends. The word echoed in her mind. Could they be friends—just casual friends?

They strolled on, absorbed in gathering shells of ivory, and bleached white hulks tinged with gold and rose, fluted amber fans, tiny brown-and-white conchs and thin, translucent, coin-sized jingoes. When Dan had gathered a great handful of jingoes, he knelt down on the sand and threaded them onto a long thin strand of seaweed.

Taking Ashly's hand, he pulled her close and with solemn ceremony, tied the ends under the golden fall of her silken hair. The gentle brush of his fingers against her skin set her pulses racing. Her heart began to pound. The necklace glowed with a lustrous, pearl-like sheen. If he had given her a string of priceless pearls, she couldn't have been more touched.

"A keepsake—a treasure from Sanibel for my lovely lady from the sea," he said, smiling down at her.

She thought of all the exquisite and expensive jewelry Werner had heaped on her. Dan's gift of this strand of shells given from the heart, touched her more deeply than all her diamonds, rubies, and pearls.

She lowered her gaze so he wouldn't see the tears that stung her eyelids. Trying to match his lighthearted tone she said, "I'll treasure it always." But her words came out in a thick, choked voice. She could say no more over the turbulent emotions churning inside her. As if he understood, he clasped her hand in his and they walked hand in hand along the bright sunlit beach in silence.

Ashly's heart ached. It wasn't fair to lead him on, to let him think there could ever be anything more between them. Then, before she lost her nerve, she blurted, "Dan, I'm serious. I really mean it. I can't see you anymore, ever."

He stopped short, staring at her with bewildered eyes. "Why?"

She swallowed hard, scarcely able to endure the wounded look in his eyes. She wanted to explain all that had happened to her, that her past haunted the present, turned her world upside down, but the words froze on her lips. At last she stammered, "I told you—I'm not going to be here much longer. I don't want to become involved with anyone, much less someone I—" She broke off abruptly. She had almost said, "Someone I care about." But that was ridiculous. She could no longer trust her own judgment and she knew it. Still, the near slip of her tongue unnerved her, for her feelings for Dan were more intense than she had realized.

He reached out and pulled her roughly into his arms. "That's no reason at all. We enjoy being together. Why not enjoy whatever time we have left?"

Tears welled in her eyes and she twisted from his grasp, crying out, "Believe me, Dan, I know what I'm doing!" She whirled away from him and stumbled across the beach, running for the sanctuary of Jessamine's cottage.

Dan, still as a pillar of stone, stood looking after her.

Ashly burst inside the cottage and shut the door then leaned against it, gasping for breath, struggling to regain her composure. She smelled brewed coffee and heard Jess and Ted chatting over breakfast on the lanai. She breathed a sigh of relief. They couldn't have seen her walking with Dan or they wouldn't have been so cheerful. Ted would be really annoyed with her after advising her not to see him again. The last thing she wanted to do was to annoy him.

Her fingers went to her throat, touching the jingo necklace. She should have thrown it away, but she wanted to keep it forever, a remembrance of Dan Kendall. She tiptoed down the hall to her room, untied the necklace, and with a pang of sadness, tucked it away under her t-shirts in a dresser drawer. She kept the junonia shell he had given her, in her pocket, curled in the palm of her hand.

Aching inside, she told herself she had done the right thing, telling Dan she couldn't see him again. It was best for both of them. Still, the pain of parting from the one person in the world who made her feel alive and well was nearly overwhelming.

The next morning she forced herself to go down to the

beach. There was no use delaying. She had to get used to being there without him, and the sooner the better. She lay down on her back and closed her eyes, trying to immerse herself in the sun's warmth, trying not to think of him, but his name filled her mind like the echo of a conch shell. A shadow touched her lids. She opened her eyes. Incredibly, as if her thoughts had conjured him up, he was standing before her, smiling down at her. She blinked, blinked again. Abruptly she sat up, shading her eyes with her hand.

He looked at her with such tenderness, that she trembled inside. "I had to see you. I knew you didn't really mean what you said yesterday. I could see it in your eyes." He hunkered down on the sand beside her.

She took a deep breath to strengthen her resolve. Squaring her shoulders, she looked directly into his eyes and stared at him without speaking, her heart too full for words. She couldn't bear to turn him away again. Couldn't explain. Couldn't say to him, "I'm not ready for love—may never be again." A warm breeze blew her hair, veiling her face, hiding the tears brimming on her eyelids.

He sat poised, waiting for what seemed endless moments, then leaned toward her and crooked a finger under her chin. With his free hand, he swept long golden strands of hair back from her face, then kissed her lightly on the forehead. Softly he said, "Think about it, Ashly." Saying no more, he got to his feet and loped away down the beach.

Despite her resolve to have no more to do with Dan, she soon discovered she had no choice, for he refused to believe her. Every day, no matter what time she chose to swim or to laze in the sun, sooner or later she would see him loping along the shore in his white t-shirt, frayed cut-offs and holey tennis shoes. At the sight of him, her heart would leap with joy. Moments later, with a boyish, good-natured smile, he would drop down beside her and start a conversation. To Ashly's astonishment, when she reminded him that she didn't want to see him anymore, far from daunted, he would reply cheerily, "I hear what you're saying," and grinning warmly, would remind her that this was a public beach.

During the days that followed, he charmed and intrigued her with tales of the island and its inhabitants: unique fish, loggerhead turtles, endangered egrets and cranes, and other wildlife that abounded on Sanibel and Captiva. He never pried into her personal life, nor did he divulge any details of his own past. Too late, she recognized that it was his very reticence that disarmed and beguiled her, made her feel that she had her emotions under control. She felt comfortable, safe, and secure whenever she was with him. He gave her a sense of well-being she had never felt, even before the Palm Air crash that haunted her. The days blended like leaves of gold, one into the other, in a euphoric blaze of sunshine, white sands, and azure waters.

A day came when Dan didn't join her. More disappointed than she would admit, she supposed he was needed at the Center. Or had he finally taken her at her word? Believed there could never be anything more between them? The next day she saw him ambling along the beach with a rag-tag crowd of young people clad in cut-offs, or bikinis. One voluptuous blonde, thin as a pencil, Ashly noted sourly, hung on his arm at every opportunity. They all boasted tans that rivaled Dan's golden oak sheen, and glowed with the energy and enthusiasm of a herd of healthy young animals. Covertly, she watched them scouring the sands, wading in the shallow surf and chatting animatedly with Dan. Envying their easy camaraderie, she longed to join them, but something held her back.

After the third morning of watching Dan and his companions cavorting on the beach, she concluded sadly, that Ted had been right. All Dan Kendall cared about was playing on the beach. She bit her lip in disappointment.

One morning after Dan's companions had deserted him and she saw him ambling along the water's edge, her curiosity got the better of her. Without thinking, she called out in teasing tones, "Don't you ever work?"

He cocked one blond brow, gazing at her with an air of

DREAM OF LOVE 45

wounded astonishment. With quick strides he closed the distance between them and sank down on the sand beside her. His dark blue gaze burned into hers. Gently he said, "I've been working all week with a group of marine biology students. They come here from various universities for a summer study program." Grinning at her, he said, "The trouble is, they keep me so busy, I can't see my little mermaid."

A surge of surprise and joy swept through her.

"That's wonderful, Dan! I had no idea you had a job other than your volunteer work at the Center."

A glimmer of amusement flickered in his eyes. "I've another job as well. Actually, I inherited a little money and a small cabin in the woods, which allows me to do what I like best."

Her interest quickened. The man was full of surprises.

"And, what I like to do best, is rescue abandoned, injured, and sick animals and birds. I keep them at the cabin till they're ready to be released. Right now I'm raising a family of otter pups whose mother deserted them."

Her face suffused with wonder, Ashly gazed up into his clean-cut, honest face. "I'd never have pegged you for a foster mother."

He gave her a rueful smile. "I also play watchdog over mad developers who charge in here with their bulldozers and level everything in sight."

Suddenly the full implication of what he was saying struck her. Understanding flashed through her mind like an explosion of light. If Dan kept track of every Sundance project, it was no wonder Ted despised him.

His voice rose, filled with enthusiasm. "And, I go to meetings to agitate for a new hurricane warning system and a new causeway. Our causeway is not only old and inadequate, but worse, it's our one and only link with the mainland. If one car breaks down on the causeway, it ties up traffic for hours. I campaign for stronger ordinances and stricter controls to prevent soil erosion and preserve our freshwater systems; and I'm involved in research projects in connection with my volunteer work at the Center."

Stunned, Ashly kept silent. The man was on a roll. She hoped he'd go on telling her of his work in his warm, eager voice. He was no beach bum, no matter what Ted said.

Suddenly contrite over her unfair judgment of him, she placed a hand on his arm. With an appealing smile, she said, "I'm impressed, Dan Kendall. I apologize for having misjudged you. It appears you have very little time to play."

Quietly he said, "I've always liked it that way." He stared directly into her bright blue eyes. "Until I met you."

His words alerted all her defenses. Their pleasant, relaxed days of fun in the sun had lulled her into a false sense of security. Without realizing it, they had become more than friends—much more. Quickly she took her hand from his arm. She absolutely would not see him again, even if she had to go into hiding.

During the days that followed, Ashly missed Dan more than she would have believed possible. It took all the courage she possessed to hide her misery behind a bright, shining smile.

Chapter 5

Ashly combed the island with Jessamine—sightseeing, shopping, luncheons—everywhere and anywhere she wouldn't see Dan. Two weeks later, on an unseasonably warm evening in February, Jessamine, looking beautiful in a seafoam green caftan, her glossy black hair braided in a coronet, sailed into the living room. At the sight of Ashly curled up in one corner of the white sectional sofa reading, she stopped short.

"Ashly, we have to leave at five-thirty. Better start dressing."

Quietly, Ashly said, "I'm not going with you tonight. I'm not into big parties."

Ted strode into the room, shrugging into a madras sport coat. "Not goin'! Ash, honey! 'Course you're goin'. We need you!"

Jessamine looked at her imploringly. "Darling, please come with us. We hate to dash off and leave you alone, and Ted is counting on you to help entertain our guests."

Ashly shook her head. "I don't mind being alone, and I'm no good at big parties and small talk."

Ted looked at her, sympathy shining in his eyes. "I know

how you feel honey—that you shouldn't be partyin' so soon after Werner's death—"

"Right!" said Ashly, too quickly. She gave a small, rueful smile. "Your friends will think I'm the merry widow of Sanibel."

Ted flung out his arms in an appealing gesture. "This isn't really a *party,* Ash. It's a business meetin'. That's all it is. The owner, Baird Seawright, will be there along with the Sundance salesmen to meet the guests who are prospective buyers, and more important, city and county officials."

Ashly wavered. City officials and monied people would be there, not beachcombers and ne'er-do-wells. Maybe it would do her good to go to a party—take her mind off Dan.

Ted went on in persuasive tones. "Listen, Ash, you don't understand how important tonight is for us. Till now, we've built only two-story condos. This is the grand openin' of our first four-story complex. We want to build three more, but everybody is givin' us a hard time—draggin' their feet over building permits. This open house in the model condo will show everyone how sensational our new development will be."

Patiently Ashly listened as Ted continued his pitch with the enthusiasm of a sideshow barker.

"We want to build a complex on the west end of Sanibel, and two more on Captiva. We have to convince these people we're not a fly-by-night outfit plannin' to throw up a bunch of tacky, prefab, high-rises that will fall apart in three years. We're creatin' a *resort,* a garden paradise, with sound, solid buildin's, beautiful landscapin', pools, golf courses, tennis courts, a resort the islands can be proud of."

Eagerly Jessamine broke in. "We need you to help us convince everyone that Sundance condos will enhance the island and give them added prestige." Her voice turned pleading. "It's only from six till nine. Please, darling, get dressed."

It sounded horrendous. Crowded, noisy, smoky, it wasn't

worth it, even to take her mind off Dan. How happy Werner would be in the center of all this festivity. For sure, Dan wouldn't be there. Still, she had no desire to go. Racking her brain for an excuse, she gave a helpless shrug. "I've nothing to wear."

"No problem," said Jessamine quickly. "I've just the thing."

Ashly sighed inwardly. Though she dreaded going, she wanted to please Jessamine and Ted. Forcing a smile, she closed her book and put it aside. "You talked me into it."

Jessamine hurried Ashly down the hall to her bedroom, plunged inside the closet and drew out a long sleeveless gown of shell pink silk that fastened on one shoulder. As she held it up to Ashly, a jubilant smile curved her lips. "Here, love, slip into this. It's perfect for you."

Laughing, Ashly exclaimed, "I can't wear that! It's much too gorgeous. It looks brand new. I can't wear your new clothes."

With an airy wave of her hand, Jessamine brushed aside her protests. "Wear it, darling. It will do magic things for you. You'll look ravishing."

Ashly eyed the gown skeptically. Jessamine had always given her good advice when they had gone clothes shopping. "Why not?" She picked up the dress and left.

Hastily she showered and dressed. The shell pink sheath complemented her long blonde hair, her startlingly light blue eyes and her golden tan. It clung to her slender figure in a way that made her appear elegant and fragile at the same time. To bolster her spirits, she dabbed a touch of perfume behind each ear. Gazing at her reflection in the mirror, it struck her that she'd feel more like herself if she wore something of her own. Quickly she rummaged through a drawer, found a pair of sparkling crystal drop earrings and put them on. When she returned to the living room where Ted and Jessamine were waiting, Ted gave a long, wolfish whistle. "Ash, honey, you've never looked more beautiful."

Jessamine beamed at her. "It's true, darling. You look like a princess."

Ashly grinned. "I feel as though I'm in disguise."

Reassured by the thought that she would see no one she knew, she held her head high and swept out the door.

Half an hour later, Ted ushered Ashly and Jessamine across a flagstone patio under a forest of hanging plants into the foyer of the crowded condo. Through a doorway on her right Ashly glimpsed a bedroom and on her left, a bright cheerful kitchen. Soft music flowed around them and the scent of perfumes mingled with the tempting aromas of hot canapés. After Jessamine and Ted introduced her to Baird Seawright and several prospective customers, Ashly wandered into the dining room to a long table laden with colorful trays of exotic fruits, salads, meats, and fish. She stopped short, captivated by the centerpiece—an ice sculpture of a seahorse riding three curling waves, set among sea fans, shells, and driftwood.

She picked up a small plate, helped herself to several hors d'oeuvres then moved on into the light, airy living room where white-coated waiters passed trays of sparkling wines and silver platters of crab claws, barbecued shrimp, smoked salmon, and toast rounds spread with cream cheese and caviar. Her admiring gaze swept over white walls, cozy loveseats and rich blue, beige, and white print draperies to a glass wall opening onto a lanai that overlooked the beach. She started up a wrought-iron stairway to explore the loft, when she heard someone call, "Ashly! Is that the real Ashly Swann?"

Her head snapped around and she let out an astonished gasp. Not ten feet away, watching her from the lanai, stood Dan Kendall. He wore a perfectly tailored blue suit, a cream-colored shirt, and was sipping a glass of white wine. His lips curved in a wide smile as he raised his glass in salute. Only his eyes gave him away. Filled with something akin to longing, they never left her face. "Come join me!"

She stood utterly still, unable to move. Her knees felt weak and she took a deep breath to steady herself. The wild thudding of her heart seemed to echo the pounding surf on the beach beneath the condo. His gaze, hot and demanding, clinging to hers, willed her to come to him. Slowly she set her plate down on a table and as though propelled by some force outside herself, moved through the crowd onto the lanai.

A faint blush tinted her cheeks as his bedazzled gaze swept her from head to toe. Softly he said, "You must be the most beautiful woman in the entire world."

Laughing softly, she shook her head. "Not so!"

"You are to me, Ashly Swann. And life without you has been pure hell."

She longed to tell him it had been hell for her too, but she didn't dare. Unable to trust herself to speak, afraid he'd see the truth in her eyes, she lowered her gaze.

He set down his glass and took both her hands in his. The warm, firm touch of his flesh imprisoning hers made her knees go weak and her fingers felt like molten wax.

Softly, he asked, "Have you missed me—just a little?"

"I—I've been busy, going places with Jessamine." Her voice trembled and she looked up then, to see if he'd noticed.

His hands tightened on hers. "You don't have to answer."

She felt hot color flooding her neck, rising up into her face. Quickly she changed the subject. "This is the last place I'd expect to see you. I thought you hated the condo crowd."

He gave a short bitter laugh. "The fact is, I was *invited*. Invited by Baird Seawright himself, I suspect to win me over." His next words were laced with sarcasm. "To see and hear what the giant developers are going to come up with next to destroy our fragile barrier islands."

Ashly tensed, and withdrew her hands from his. "Dan, be fair. Sundance builds beautiful, structurally sound condos, and the grounds, landscaped as a luxury resort, will look far more beautiful than they do today. My brother-in-law hopes the islanders will be so impressed with this complex that they'll approve future plans."

Dan's bronzed, rugged features hardened. "This complex is sure to attract hordes of bird-brained tourists who will ruin the island they came to see."

Nearby guests turned toward Dan and Ashly with curious expressions. Others, who evidently felt the tension in the air, fell silent.

An angry voice sliced through the highly charged atmosphere. "And without those tourists, your island will die!"

Ashly whirled to see Ted red-faced, glowering at Dan. Ted stepped forward, facing Dan head on. "Those tourists you despise support the local economy so that parasites like you can live here!" His voice rose, loud and defiant. "Furthermore, Sundance buyers are not tourists. They're property owners who are as eager as you are to preserve the island. Your trouble is, you want to keep the place for yourself and others like you, so you and your good-for-nothing friends can go on livin' without doing a lick of work to justify your existence!"

In low, hard tones, Dan replied, "It's none of your damn business what I do or how I live."

Ashly winced, mentally scoring a point for Dan.

"The fact is," Dan continued, "I *do* live here and intend to stay, if we can keep you and your company from destroying the islands."

Other guests crowded through the doorway onto the lanai, staring, asking in excited voices what was happening. Ashly saw Baird Seawright watching intently from the back of the room, as though poised to step in if the argument got too far out of hand. Someone turned down the music, the better to hear the discussion, Ashly supposed.

Dan, in total command of himself and the situation, glared at Ted. In low, taut tones, he said, "So you mind your business, and I'll mind mine."

"Make damn sure you do!" Ted snapped. "It's time you stopped meddlin' in things that don't concern you!"

Diamond-hard light flashed in Dan's eyes. "The ecology

of this island concerns me greatly. It's too bad that it doesn't concern you as well."

He turned and strode from the lanai through the dining room into the living room as if to leave. Ted followed close on his heels. Swiftly Ashly joined them.

"Listen to me, Kendall."

Dan halted, and spun to face him.

"We have trouble enough with the city council changin' the zoning laws, denyin' buildin' permits. So stick to your beachcombing and forget Sundance Resorts!"

Ashly stiffened, her throat tightened. Forgetting Sundance was the last thing Dan would do. Red-faced, furious, shouting, they stood nose to nose, toe to toe, like two fighting cocks.

Arguments always unnerved her, especially between people she loved, and this one was fast heading toward a full-fledged fight. She couldn't bear to listen one second longer, couldn't stand to watch it erupt before her eyes. She dashed through the living room, up the stairs to the loft. With a feeling of dread, she leaned over the banister and surveyed the room below.

An excited hum like the buzzing of bees rose from the guests. Jessamine strode regally through the crowd, as guests drew back, opening a path for her. She approached the men, linked one arm through Dan's right arm, the other through Ted's left arm and escorted them into the dining room. Spellbound, the guests fell silent. So softly that everyone had to strain to hear her, Jessamine said, "Gentlemen, the time has come to speak of other things."

Ashly went into the bedroom and closed the door. She sank down on the bed and took long deep breaths until her heart slowed its beating and she began to relax. Still, she felt torn apart by conflicting loyalties. She could see Ted's point, but she had to admire Dan for taking a stand against him.

The sound of music and laughter drifted up to the loft from the lanai below. The party was going full-tilt. She breathed a sigh of relief. Thank God the men had apparently settled their quarrel. Knowing Jessamine would wonder what had become of her, she started to go downstairs to mingle with the guests. Then, from the corner of her eye she caught a glint of lamplight on the brass doorknob as it slowly turned and the door swung open. Had Dan dared to seek her out? She held her breath, then let it out in a rush.

Ted, looking sheepish and apologetic, dropped down onto a ladderback chair across from Ashly. He leaned forward, bracing his elbows on his knees, his hands clasped between them. "Sorry about the blow-up, Ash, honey, but someone had to shut Kendall up."

Ashly's blond brows lifted in wry amusement. "And *did* you shut him up?"

Ted scowled irritably. "Jessamine did. Thank God he had enough sense to get the hell out of here. I just hope he hasn't blown the whole project sky-high with all his conservation prattle. He knew damn well we were givin' this party to gain support for Sundance Resorts. So this—this hop-head starts spoutin' off all the reasons why the city should send us packin'. I'd like to put a muzzle on that guy!"

Ashly suppressed a grin. Ted, who had always been able to persuade anyone of anything with a smile and a handshake had met his match. "Did anyone important hear him?"

"How could they help hearin' him?" Ted ran his hands distractedly through his fine brown hair. "Will they *listen* to him, that's the question."

Without thinking, she rose to Dan's defense. "He was *invited* here, you know."

Ted looked at her in astonishment. "He wasn't on *my* invitation list."

"I imagine Baird Seawright had in mind to give him his number one sales pitch. Try to convince him to chill out."

"Huh! I'd like to run him clear off the island!"

It was on the tip of her tongue to tell Ted that he'd stir

up a hornet's nest if he tried to run off the director of the Nature Center. And she wanted to tell him why Dan was so concerned with the ecology of the island and so, understandably, opposed to any construction he thought would upset nature's balance, but she bit back the words. Defending Dan would only inflame Ted further. After all, Ted and Jessamine had stood by her throughout all the terrible days of grief and remorse after the tragedy; had offered her a haven when she so badly needed it. How could she take take a stand against them?

Ted gazed at her, a thoughtful frown creasing his brow. "The man appears attracted to you, and now I see what he's up to, tryin' to win you over to his side, tryin' to get to me through you. Thank God I warned you away from him from the start."

Ashly felt a stab of annoyance. Why should Ted think Dan's feelings for her were purely self-interest? He was honestly attracted to her. The warm way he looked at her told her that. His genuine concern when he thought she was drowning, the worried look in his eyes when she'd almost cut her hand on the rough grass, his eagerness to spend time with her, all showed he cared. Defensively, she burst out, "Do you realize that Dan Kendall is the only friend I have on the entire island?"

Ted's mouth curved in a reassuring smile. "You'll soon make other friends. It doesn't look good for a Sundance sales manager to have a shiftless beachcomber hangin' around, gleanin' information to stir up the residents. Now that you know what he's up to, steer clear of him." His bright gray eyes filled with sympathy. "I know how hard it is for you, here in a strange town, know how lonely you must feel, but in time, livin' here with Jess and me, that will pass."

Touched by Ted's words, unwanted tears shimmered in Ashly's eyes. "I hadn't planned to see him again."

Ted, who could never stand to see a woman cry, put his arms around her shoulders in a comforting hug. "Ash, honey, remember, Jess and I are goin' to look after you always. All we want is to make you happy."

Ashly closed her eyes and nodded, making no reply. A feeling of depression enveloped her like a shroud.

Chapter 6

Ashly woke to bright morning sunlight with a strong sense of urgency, of something she must do, now. She sat up and squinted at her watch through eyes puffy from lack of sleep. Ten-fifteen. All night long she had rolled and tossed and now she had overslept. Ted's talk of "taking care of her always" had upset her more than his angry confrontation with Dan, and filled her with alarm. What she wanted more than anything in this world was to fly again. She missed the travel, the new faces, and the camaraderie of the flight crews.

She had never intended to stay here forever. She had hoped that an interlude at Sanibel would help her conquer the trauma that haunted her days and nights. Now she was beginning to hope. The anger she had once felt had abated. And more than three weeks had passed without a nightmare or flashback. Were they gone for good? If so, she no longer had a reason to stay with Jess and Ted. With a small shock, it struck her that unwittingly, Jessamine and Ted were making life too pleasant for her. It would be too easy to fall into the pattern of their lives, to forfeit her independence, to escape reality. She gave a deep sigh. Painful though it would be, she knew what she must do.

Having made a decision, she was eager to get on with it. First, she would tell Jessamine, then go to see Dan. She wanted to tell him goodbye, that she was leaving Sanibel Island for good.

She showered, donned a raspberry gauze shirt and white cotton skirt, brushed her hair until it glinted with golden lights and bound it at the back of her neck with a pink silk scarf. Feeling as though she were preparing to do battle, she put on lipstick and dabbed perfume behind each ear. Impulsively, she slid the junonia shell in her pocket.

Walking toward the lanai, she heard Jessamine and Ted chatting amiably over the breakfast table. She had expected Ted to be gone by now. Frowning, she turned back to her room. She would wait to tell Jessamine until they were alone. Ted would never understand her leaving. She paced her room until she heard his Mercedes crunching down the shell driveway, then hurried down the hall to the lanai.

Jessamine, seated at the table, smiled a greeting and put down the paper she was reading. "Pancakes or waffles?"

Feeling driven and tense over what she had to do, Ashly's stomach knotted. "Just coffee, thanks." She filled a mug from the carafe and sat down across from Jessamine. Taking a deep breath she looked her sister directly in the eyes.

"Jessamine, I have something to tell you."

Jessamine's eyes widened in sympathy. "Of course, darling. You know I'm always ready to listen."

Ashly, thinking an indirect approach was kinder, decided to tell her why, before she told her what she was going to do. Gently, she said, "The trouble is, Ted seems to think I need constant comforting and consoling; that it's his mission in life to look after me. I don't need looking after, Jess. The truth is, I feel I'm imposing. So I've decided that—"

Jessamine waved a slender hand in dismissal. "Forget it,

darling. Ted loves looking after you. Loves having you here."

Ashly set her mug down hard and leaned toward Jessamine. "But I don't *mind* being alone. I *want* to be left alone."

A warm, loving expression shone from Jessamine's eyes. "Don't be silly, darling. It's Ted's nature. He's a very loving, caring man. Don't take him so seriously."

Taking another deep breath, Ashly plunged on. "I understand. It's just Ted's way. And I know his intentions are the best, but he's killing me with kindness."

Jessamine gave a small, rueful laugh. "To be honest with you, I have the same problem. Ted can't see a need, real or imagined, without trying to fill it. He wants everyone around him to be happy. Everything he's done since the day we were married has been to make me happy." Her face grew grave and she leaned toward Ashly, palms outstretched, as if pleading for understanding. "The thing is, all I've ever really wanted is a home of my own with polished furniture, gleaming silver and china, and flowers on the table—"

Ashly smiled fondly at her. "What a romantic you are."

"I'm serious, Ashly. I won't deny I enjoyed the money and fame that modeling brought me. But all I've ever really wanted is to make a home for a husband I love and cherish, a husband who loves and cherishes me."

Ashly stared at her dismayed. "You have all that, Jess."

An expression of anxiety crossed the smooth perfection of Jessamine's features. She rested her arms on the table, lacing her long slender fingers tightly together.

"I gave up my career willingly because I loved Ted and wanted to marry him. Now I want to have his children. I want to feel like a *family*."

Ashly's brows rose. "Well, why not?"

"Listen, Ashly, *Ted's* life is exactly the way he wants it. He's a scratch golfer, an 'A' tennis player, sails, fishes, mingles with the rich and famous who come to Sanibel. Women flock around him like bees to a honeypot." An indulgent laugh escaped her. "That isn't the problem. He tells me no woman in the world can hold a candle to me; says pleasing potential buyers is our bread and butter. And he wants me to be involved in all the social and civic activities on the island, says it's good public relations for Sundance." Her voice rose in agitation. "Well, I understand all that, but this isn't enough for me. I could be happy here—" she paused and a look of longing so intense that Ashly could scarcely endure it came into her eyes, "if only we had a child."

Ashly's heart turned over. Until this moment, she'd always thought Jessamine had everything she could want. "Well?" she asked quietly.

Jessamine gave a hopeless shake of her head. "At first Ted insisted we wait to start a family till we were on our feet financially. After he got this fantastic job with Sundance whenever I mentioned having a baby, he shrugged and said, later—maybe." Anxiety clouded her eyes. "Suppose something happens to Ted, like—" She broke off, an appalled expression on her face. At once contrite, her soft blue eyes filled with compassion. "Sorry, Ashly. That was stupid of me."

Ashly knew she was thinking: *Werner gone, leaving poor Ashly without even the comfort of a child.* An aching sympathy for Jessamine rose inside her. Gently she asked, "And what do you say to Ted's, 'Later—maybe'?"

"Later is now."

"Now?"

"I'm pregnant."

Ashly's eyes lighted with joy. "Oh, Jess, I'm so happy for you." Ashly jumped up from her chair, threw her arms around Jessamine and gave her a loving hug. "When's your due date?"

"Mid-July."

"July!" She did a quick figuring, "You must have gotten pregnant last October. You've known all this time, and you never breathed a word. How could you keep quiet?"

"I wanted to wait a few months to be absolutely sure,

and to make sure nothing went wrong. I felt so rotten at the beginning. That's why I kept begging you to come to see us."

"Have you told Ted?"

Silently, she nodded.

"Well, wasn't he thriled?"

"Hardly."

"Surely you can afford to have a child now."

Ashly gave a resigned sigh. "True. But I'm afraid the real problem is that Ted can't stand the competition of a child. He wants to be all things to me." Her voice turned hoarse and dry. "Ted really doesn't want children, Ashly. He wants me to have an abortion."

For a moment Ashly sat frozen, numb with shock. Then leaning across the table, she took Jessamine's arm in a firm grip. "Jessamine, no. He can't mean that. You said he wants you to be happy. An abortion would be crazy, would solve nothing."

Jessamine jerked her arm from Ashly's grasp in a defensive gesture. "It's more complicated than that!"

Softly, pleading, Ashly said, "Ted will come around. You'll see."

Jessamine sighed deeply. "No. He doesn't want a child."

Her heart ached for Jessamine. Desperately she searched for the right words to keep her sister from throwing love away, from doing something she could regret the rest of her life. "Listen to me, Jessamine. Ted's never had a child. Judging by the way he tries to look after us, what he needs most in this world is someone to take care of. Believe me!"

Jessamine smiled wistfully. "I wish I could."

Ashly said, "Listen to me, Jess. You're going to have that baby. If Ted doesn't want it, I'll take it."

Jessamine gave a feeble laugh. "I'll think about it."

"No!" Ashly slammed a fist down on the table. "Listen to me Jessamine. Do not even *think* about having an abortion."

"Actually, I hate to think about it." She heaved a huge

sigh. "Maybe the baby will be a boy. Maybe he will look just like Ted. Maybe then Ted will love it."

"You *will* have this baby," Ashly said forcefully. "Right?"

Jessamine gave her a long, level look, as though considering.

"Promise?" Ashly persisted.

Jessamine nodded.

"No guts, no glory. Right?"

"Right!" As if eager to end a painful discussion, Jessamine glanced at her watch and stood up. "Good heavens, it's ten-thirty, and I promised to help with the book sale today. I have to fly!"

For some moments after Jessamine left, Ashly sat unmoving, her mind spinning over Jessamine's revelation. This was why her sister had seemed so distracted and preoccupied. Slowly Ashly sipped her coffee. Jessamine, far from reassuring her that she wasn't imposing, had only convinced her further that Jess and Ted needed time to be alone, time for loving.

Ten minutes later Ashly was pedaling down the bicycle path along the San-Cap Road. She glanced worriedly at the sky overhead, and the dark gray clouds that concealed it. She pedaled harder. If only she could speak with Dan privately, before he took the visitors on the nature tour.

No doubt he was furious with Ted, after their confrontation last night. Would his anger carry over to Ted's family? Would he be angry with her as well? When she told him she was leaving Sanibel, would he be glad or disappointed? Neither, she decided dully. Why should he care?

Dashing inside the Nature Center, Ashly glanced at her watch. Five after eleven. Anxiously she scanned the lobby. No tour group waited before the glass doors. Her heart turned over. Breathless, upset, she bumped headlong into Martha Kirby. Her face turned scarlet. "Sorry, Martha. I was hurrying to catch the tour before they left."

Martha shook her head. "Left five minutes ago."

A pinched, frozen look came over Ashly's face. "I wanted to see Dan before he took off."

Smiling warmly, Martha nodded. "No problem. Chris Alexander is on tour duty today. Dan is interviewing someone in his office, but he'll be out any minute." She sank down on a wooden bench and patted a place beside her. "I'll keep you company while you wait."

Ashly sat down, and fishing a bill from her skirt pocket, pressed it into Martha's hand. "I want to give you this—my admission fee."

Her mind on Dan, Ashly listened abstractedly to Martha's amiable gossip until she heard her saying, ". . . one of those petite, dark-eyed brunettes, set her cap for Dan, but he'd have none of her."

Ashly grinned. "I'm amazed that a man as attractive as Dan isn't married."

Martha's bright eyes drkened. "He *was* married. Quite happily. But his wife died about three years ago."

Tears of sympathy sprang to Ashly's eyes. "Yes, I heard." Again she felt a sudden kinship with Dan, although, the feeling unnerved her.

Martha interrupted her thoughts. "There he is now! And there he goes!"

Ashly looked up and saw his lean, tanned figure in red t-shirt and khaki slacks, striding out through the glass doors. She jumped to her feet and ran after him. He was standing just outside the door peering inside the weathered nesting box mounted on the wall.

"Dan," she said softly. Her voice caught in her throat.

He turned toward her. A smile of mingled pleasure and surprise lighted his face.

"This is my lucky day!"

Thank heaven he was glad to see her, she thought, not holding a grudge because of Ted. Ironically, she didn't want to tell him what she'd come to say. It was harder than she'd imagined, too hard. Cheeks flaming, she said, "I wanted to tell you, I'm sorry about what happened yesterday. Ted really is a good person, he's just—"

"Just ill-informed." Dan reached out and brushed her cheek with a gentle hand. "No apology needed. But I'm glad you came." He turned back to the nesting box. "Look, I want to show you something." He reached inside the box, drew out several feathers and held them in the palm of his hand. In elated tones he said, "They appear fresh. I think our itinerant barn owl has nested."

Ashly could have cried with relief. Clearly he was totally fascinated with his barn owl, and couldn't care less about Ted LeBeau. He picked up a short, stiff brown feather and turned it over, examining it closely.

A small, insistent voice inside her shouted, "Tell him. Tell him now!" In tremulous tones, she said, "Dan, I want to talk to you."

He placed the feather carefully on top of the box and turned to face her. "Sounds serious."

She turned from him and ran onto the boardwalk bridge. Her eyes shimmered with unwanted tears as she stared down into the dark swamp of spartina grass.

He stood silent and unmoving, watching her with a baffled expression. A sudden ray of sunshine highlighted the long golden hair streaming down her back. Fine wisps escaped her pink scarf and lay along the slender curve of her neck making her appear soft and delicate and terribly vulnerable. From the corner of her eye she saw in his face a tenderness she'd never seen before. Her throat constricted, so that she couldn't speak. Her courage deserted her.

Slowly, head down, shoulders drooping, she walked away from him, down the dappled sunlit path, deep into the woodland. As she emerged in a clearing on the edge of the riverbank, she felt strong fingers close over her left shoulder. The next instant Dan swung her around to face him then drew her close, locking his hands at the small of her slender back. When he spoke, his voice was husky and gentle.

"I don't know what's troubling you, sweetheart, but whatever it is, I'm on your team." He said no more, but held her tightly, smoothing her hair with his free hand.

Her arms crept up around his neck and reveling in the

shelter of his embrace, she nestled her head in the snug hollow between his chin and shoulder, pressing against his broad chest, his powerful legs braced against her own. Breathing deeply of the earthy, woodsy scent of him, she let out a long, contented sigh.

Dan curved a finger under her chin, raising her face to his. His questioning eyes held hers, until Ashly felt she was drowning in their light fathomless depths. When she still didn't speak, he bent his head to hers and his lips brushed hers in a light, feathery kiss. His breath, like fresh apples, mingled with her own and her mouth clung to his, tasting, lingering. She yearned to prolong the exquisite sweetness of this moment forever.

His arms tightened around her, crushing her tightly against his chest. The frantic pounding of her heart matched the swift beat of his, pressed to her own. For endless moments they stood entwined, the sun beating down on them, searing their bodies, stirring their blood.

Their kisses deepened, feverish, frantic, seeking. Dan loosened her thin shirt from its restraining waistband and slid his hand upward, stroking the soft fullness of her breasts, teasing the taut rosebud nipples. Giddy with delight at his touch, Ashly swayed in his arms. Minutes raced past as their hunger for each other mounted. She ran her fingers through his hair, caressed the back of his neck, ran her hands up and down his back, urging him closer, as if to fuse their bodies together as one.

Dimly, in the distance, Ashly heard voices. She stirred, drawing back within the circle of his arms. In a tremulous whisper, she murmured, "Dan, someone's coming."

His lips brushed her earlobe. His voice was low and husky. "They're on another trail. Won't come near us."

His mouth took hers once more with rising passion, demanding.

Her lips clinging to his, she murmured, "But they'll see us through the trees."

Dan backed away, glanced around them. Through narrowed lids, his gaze swept past an osprey nest mounted on a tall pole, a stand of pepper trees, scattered cactus and scrub. As he looked down over Ashly's shoulder, she felt his body stiffen. His lips curved in a crooked grin. Lightly he said, "Shall we dance?" Without waiting for her reply, he pulled her close against him. Smiling into her eyes, softly humming a romantic tune, he swung her along the shaded path in a slow waltz.

Ashly craned her neck, tried to peer over her shoulder, but he clamped one large hand back of her head, holding it still. Firmly he said, "Just follow along with me." He began to hum again.

The romantic words sang in her head. Sorrowfully, she thought, this is it. This is the last time Dan and I will ever be together. She felt hot tears forming in her eyes. To break the spell, she looked up into his face and laughed softly. "If anyone sees us, they'll think we're out of our minds, dancing in the woods."

Dan smiled, and made no reply.

She stepped lightly, her footsteps matching his, feeling feather-light in his arms. After several moments he swung her around so that she stood with her back to him, facing down the path. He held her shoulders in a firm clasp. She wished his strong hands, so warm and reassuring, would clasp her shoulders forever.

As they rambled down the winding woodland path along the ridge, catching occasional glimpses of the river, her heart still pounded from his burning kisses, the tingling thrill of his embrace. She had behaved scandalously, she thought, smiling to herself. But Dan's swift change of mood, from the ardor of their passions to a frivolous impulse to dance, puzzled her. With an amused twinkle in her eyes, she looked at him over her shoulder. "Why the minute waltz, Dan?"

A peculiar light came into his eyes. He shook his head and said quietly, "Don't talk. You'll frighten the animals and you might miss seeing something wonderful."

Ashly's curiosity continued to prickle, and when they came to a break in the trees, she strolled off the trail to

DREAM OF LOVE 67

the riverbank. Shading her eyes with her hand, she followed the course of the shiny brown waters to the clearing where they had been standing when Dan took her in his arms to waltz. As her eyes raked the bank, she clapped a hand to her mouth. Perspiration sprang out on her forehead and a cold tremor crept up her spine. In a voice that shook, she said, "I see why we were waltzing so blithely along the trail." Gooseflesh rose on her arms and the back of her neck as she gazed down on a ten-foot, leathery brown alligator lazing in the sun.

Amusement lighted his eyes. "He likes to snooze during the day. Remember, I said 'gators won't attack if you don't bother them. I was afraid you'd start screeching and wake him up." A warning note came into his voice. "Mustn't disturb the animals."

Ashly closed her eyes and as if speaking a solemn vow, said, "I wouldn't disturb him for the world. But it sounds as if you'd save the animals first and people last."

Dan grinned, his blond brows lifting as if in consideration. "Not a bad idea. Not bad at all."

Ashly grinned back at him. "Now I know where I stand."

Laughing, Dan took her hand and led her along the path. Her hand trembled in his, and his grip tightened. He smiled down at her. "You can relax. The 'gator's forgotten all about us."

She said nothing, thinking uneasily that she had not forgotten the alligator; nor had she forgotten the way Dan stirred her emotions into fires which had nearly blazed out of control. It struck her then that she was unsure which was more dangerous: the alligator or Dan Kendall. Without warning, a surge of guilt flooded through her, the guilt that had tormented her ever since the tragedy, engulfing her.

When they reached the Center, instead of going inside, Dan led her across the crushed shell parking area and halted beside a battered red MG. Still holding her hand tightly, he said, "This afternoon the Center is featuring a special program on butterflies."

It struck her then that she hadn't told him what she had come to say. She took a deep breath. With an effort of will, she forced the words. "Dan, I'm sorry. I can't stay for your program. I just want to tell you . . ."

As if she hadn't spoken, he wrenched open the car door and handed her inside. *"I'm* not giving the program. One of our volunteers is—a butterfly expert. I'm not needed here this afternoon."

She placed a hand on his arm and in no-nonsense tones said, "Listen, Dan, I have something to tell you—"

Smiling down at her, he said, "Tell me later. Now I'm taking you on a personally escorted tour of Captiva Island."

"Captiva!" she echoed wistfully. *"Tell him,"* said a small voice inside her head. *"Tell him what you have to say, and go."* Instead, she said, "I've been dying to see the island, but we've never had time."

Whether a cloud veiled the sun, or it was a trick of the sunlight sifting through the trees, she couldn't tell, but a shadow passed over Dan's usually cheerful features. He stood quite still, one hand gripping the car door, gazing deeply into her eyes.

"There's never enough time, Ashly. Never enough time for everything." Abruptly he slammed the door and as he did so, she saw pain in his eyes, deep and haunting. She longed to heal it.

Chapter 7

Seated beside Dan in the MG, with the top down, Ashly reveled in the soft salt breeze blowing her hair, cooling her cheeks. Confined in the small car, intensely aware of Dan's long, lean frame so close to her side, her heart beat a fast tattoo. She watched him from the corner of her eye. The golden sheen of his skin made her yearn to run her fingertips down the line of his cheek, along his strong, stubborn jaw. Afraid he'd see desire mirrored in her eyes, she glanced away. Slipping a hand in her pocket, she clenched the junonia. Charmed by his deep, resonant voice, she returned her attention to what he was saying.

"Captiva is only about six miles long and one-quarter to one mile wide. Actually, the two islands form a crescent, connected by a short bridge, with Sanibel at the lower end."

He threw her a sidelong glance, his lips curved in a wicked grin. "Legend has it that more than two hundred years ago a buccaneer, Jose Gaspar, sailed up San Carlos Bay and anchored at Captiva. Here, Gaspar and his marauding pirate crew hid out, living it up on the white beaches and warm gulf waters. They say he buried his treasure here and, more important, built a compound where he imprisoned countless beautiful women, captives from pirate forays."

A teasing light sparkled in Ashly's eyes. "Do you suppose those things still happen?"

Dan grinned. "Today? I'd be tempted, if you were the beautiful woman."

How would it feel, she wondered, to be held captive by Dan Kendall? A shiver of delight ran up her spine as she relived the ecstasy of their passionate embrace on the riverbank, his kisses searing her throbbing lips. How would it feel to lie in his arms all through the long, dark, lonely nights? To be the one to arouse the fiery passions she suspected lay hidden beneath his easy-going exterior? Startled by the intensity of her desire for him, she told herself firmly that it was foolish to indulge in such fantasies. She must stop at once. Grateful that he couldn't hear the wild beating of her heart, she kept her voice light.

"Tell me some more. I like history."

"Well, geologists say Sanibel began as a sandspit at the southern end of Captiva about 3,000 B.C. Indian mounds found in the Wulfert area indicate occupation between 500 B.C. to A.D. 1. And more recently, radio carbon dating shows evidence of an Indian civilization around A.D. 1200. Probably predecessors of the Caloosa civilization."

"Jessamine told me Sanibel was named Santa Isybella in honor of Queen Isabella."

Dan shook his head. "Ellie Dormer, one of our most respected local historians, says that's sheer fiction. She found a 1765 map of the island that shows a harbor labeled Puerto de S. Nivel. Later an official Spanish map dated 1768 turned up which identifies Sanibel as Puerto de S. Nibel. 'S' can mean 'saint,' and 'v' and 'b' are interchangeable, so the name was corrupted from Sn. Nibel to Sanibel."

Smiling, Ashly nodded. "I'll settle for that."

They rode in companionable silence enjoying the scenery as the small red MG sped past plumed Australian pines, sabal palms and seagrape trees, weathered frame cottages, a school, a fire station, and a shopping center. Soon they emerged from the woodland and crossed a narrow bridge that spanned blue-green water edged by a bleached white sandy shore.

"Blind Pass Bridge," remarked Dan amiably. "We're on Captiva."

Swimmers and sunbathers sprawled on the beach. Others swarmed about an open-sided white truck parked under a shade tree where a man hawked pizza and sandwiches.

"Looks like fun," said Ashly smiling.

Dan turned to look at her, his eyes crinkled with amusement. "Much too crowded!"

She made no reply, but gazed around her enthralled, breathing deeply of the fragrant scent of pine. The road grew bumpy, and the MG rocketed past a huge yellow tractor rolling over fresh blacktop on the far side of the road. Small neat signs marked driveways that led to private homes hidden deep in the woodland. As they sped along the shore road the trees thinned. A row of Australian pines bent like archer's bows toward the green Gulf waters that shaded to a sparkling aqua. A ruler-straight line marked the horizon and above it hung a vast dome of pastel blue sky.

Ashly watched enchanted as they drove through the charming old town past colorful frame houses, stores bustling with people, and bicycle riders with orange pennants fluttering from thin poles mounted on their fenders.

Dan pulled up before a row of brown-timbered, rustic-looking shops bordered by a wide wooden balcony. Crimson hibiscus spilled over the railing. At the far end stood wooden tables and chairs. A sign read: CAFÉ CAPTIVA.

He opened the car door and handed her out. Cheerfully, he said, "The Café serves some of the best food on the island." His warm gaze swept over her slender figure. "I plan to ply you with food and drink, so watch out."

Ashly grinned up at him. "Terrific!"

As they mounted the steps, Dan clasped her arm lightly

and tiny shock waves tingled through her. She curled her fingers tightly around the junonia in her pocket.

They sat at a table beside a huge seagrape tree from which fluttered rust-colored, plate-shaped leaves. Nearby stood clusters of sabal palms and a riot of brilliant scarlet and purple bougainvillea. A sleepy-eyed, bearded young waiter took their order: a glass of white wine and the house sandwich for Ashly; and a beer and barbecued beef for Dan.

A sudden silence fell between them and her edgy feeling of the early morning returned. After dashing off to the Center hellbent on telling Dan what she had decided to do, now she was holding back. Why? Was she unwilling to follow through or was she simply reluctant to say the words that would bring this lovely interlude to an end? Neither, she told herself firmly. She had only been waiting for the right moment. Still she sat silent, watching him.

He took a deep swallow of beer and leaned back in his chair, relaxing. A contented smile lighted his features.

Now, Ashly told herself. Now is the time. Go! As if on signal, a sudden roar shattered the peaceful silence of the sunny afternoon. Her head snapped around. Across the road on a field shorn of trees, a gigantic yellow pile driver was driving piles into the ground with resounding fury.

Dan's eyes blazed, his features contorted in a fierce glare. "There they go!" he shouted above the din. "All in the name of progress! If builders keep on despoiling the island with their glass and steel, there won't be a square foot of ground left to stand on, and what's here will sink into the Gulf!"

Ashly nodded, bracing herself, shutting out the ear-splitting racket of clashing metal. Dan couldn't hear her if she shouted at the top of her lungs. An omen? Maybe she needn't *tell* Dan, just send him a goodbye note. But she knew better.

They ate and drank, smiling at each other with their eyes. Ashly had finished the last delicious bite of her sandwich, dark raisin bread with layers of cream cheese, pineapple, sliced tomatoes, and cucumber, and Dan had downed a thick, barbecued pork sandwich before the piledrivers finally took a break and they could make themselves heard. In the shock of the sudden silence, Ashly took a deep breath and without preamble said, "Dan, I'm leaving Sanibel."

He couldn't have looked more stunned if she'd told him the island would sink into the Gulf by sundown. After a long moment he lifted the frosty beer to his lips and drank deeply, as though giving himself time to frame a reply. Carefully, deliberately, he set down the can. A deep scowl furrowed his brow. He ran his hands through his hair then rested his elbows on the table, his chin in his hands. "That's the worst news I've heard all day."

Seeing mingled reproach and disappointment reflected in his eyes, Ashly shrank inside. She straightened, squared her shoulders, and met his gaze head on. Her throat tightening with the effort of forcing out words she hated to say. "It's the only thing to do."

"Why? Why leave, when you have everything going for you?"

Ashly gave a vehement shake of her head, and a cascade of golden hair swept across her face, hiding her anguished expression. "Everything isn't going for me. I realized that yesterday." A bleak expression came into her eyes. "Ted's 'big brother' routine is getting to me. He can't help being the way he is and he's going to keep on 'taking care of me,' whether I need it or not. In the end, I'll still have to leave." Suppressing a sigh, she went on.

"Anyway, now is the ideal time to go. Jessamine won't be lonely much longer. She's pregnant."

Dan brightened. "Hey. That's good news, isn't it?"

"*I* think so."

"Won't she need your help?"

"If she does, I can always go back. Anyway, a guest should leave before she wears out her welcome."

A closed, set expression came over Dan's features. "But you're not a guest, for Pete's sake."

Softly she said, "Three's a crowd."

"I get the picture. But if Ted is too solicitous, why not tell him to back off?"

"I *have* told him, several times, that I don't need him hovering over me," said Ashly miserably. "He says he understands, but after a few days he forgets." A rueful grin twisted her lips. "It's his nature, trying to keep the people he loves happy all the time."

Dan cocked a bristly blond eyebrow at her. "Then have Jessamine give him the word."

Ashly sighed, her shoulders sagging in defeat. "I've told Jessamine that Ted is too, too much, that all I want is to be left alone. Jessamine said I was being silly; that this is just Ted's way; that he doesn't feel one bit put upon, or that I'm taking her time away from him."

The corners of his mouth turned down in a grimace. "Good old Ted, swept out to sea on his ship of good intentions!"

"It's no good your making a joke of it," she said over a lump in her throat. She gave a hopeless shake of her head, flinging her bright mane over her shoulder. "It's time for me to move on, to find a place to live, and some kind of job." She thought, but did not say, *Until Palm Air will let me fly again.*

"Flying?"

She shook her head.

Dan reached across the table and covered her slender hands with his, holding them in a strong, comforting grasp. A feeling of warmth and confidence seemed to flow from his hands into hers. Softly he said, "Why not work here on Sanibel? Then you can still see your sister."

Ashly flushed, acutely aware of his hands covering hers, of the fine golden hairs that curled on their tanned backs. She withdrew her hands from his, slid one hand in her pocket, and clutched the junonia tightly. Her mind reeled. If she stayed, she would also see Dan. It was tempting, so tempting. But she was far from ready for love.

She looked up, meeting his expectant gaze. "No, I can't

stay. I've looked over help-wanted ads in the paper. There are only a few jobs—waitresses, clerks, sitters—which I could fill. And I checked apartment ads too. Rents are sky-high, much more than I could afford. I love Sanibel, but the price of paradise is too high." Her lips curved in a rueful smile. Her throat ached horribly, but she forced herself to go on. "I have to go back to the real world sometime. Now is the time."

She turned abruptly to stare at the bougainvillea, so he wouldn't see the sudden tears stinging her eyelids. The crimson and purple blossoms shimmered in the soft, warm air. Swiftly she rose from the table. As she did so, something slid from her lap, struck the floor, but she couldn't stop. On legs that shook, she ran down the long wooden balcony, down the stairs to the MG. As she sank onto the warm leather seat, the pile-drivers resumed their deafening pounding. With each stroke she felt as though the shining steel piles were being driven into her heart.

Through brimming eyes, Ashly saw Dan rise from his chair with the air of a prizefighter struggling to his feet after a knock-out blow, saw him bend over and scoop up something from the floor. He straightened and opening his hand, stared down at his palm, an inscrutable expression on his clean-cut features. Ashly leaned forward, inclining her head to see. A beam of sunlight slanting through the trees glinted off the satin-smooth surface of the junonia on Dan's palm. Inexplicably, Ashly felt like bursting into tears.

Chapter 8

Dan, hunched over the wheel of the MG, staring straight ahead, drove through the picturesque streets of Captiva in dour silence.

When Ashly's heart finally settled down to its normal, steady beating, she resolved to act as though nothing had happened to spoil their warm camaraderie. Now, unable to endure Dan shutting her out a minute longer, she asked softly, "Aren't you going to speak to me again?"

"No." He continued to stare at the road as if peering through a thick fog, though there was nothing ahead but clear, pure air shimmering in the brilliant sunlight.

Ashly turned to face him. "You must see that I'm right."

"I'm thinking."

"Private thoughts?"

"Very private."

Ashly sank back in the seat feeling as though he had slammed a door in her face. He had a right to refuse to share his thoughts with her. *She'd* refused to share *her* thoughts—couldn't, wouldn't speak of her past. She dreaded to think of it, much less talk about it. To speak of it would bring back all the pain and horror she was trying so hard to forget. Dan too could keep his thoughts to himself. Still, feeling shut out, she retreated into her shell.

As the silence between them lengthened, she stole a glance at him to etch his profile on her memory for all time. Thick, tousled, sun-bleached hair crowning a broad brow furrowed in thought. Straight, strong nose and stubborn jutting jaw. Full sensuous lips that could be meltingly warm and tender, now clamped in a thin line. Soon she would be gone, never to see him again. The thought made her heart swell with pain. With trembling fingers she retied the pink scarf that bound her hair, then forced her attention back to the passing scene, the quaint shops and charming cottages that graced the streets of the old town.

Dan slowed the MG and swung onto Chapin Street. As they passed a white wooden building on the right, he murmured, "Captiva Library."

Unexpectedly, at the next driveway he turned in and parked before a small white frame church nestled in the shade of a lacy Australian pine. A trim blue and white sign read: "Chapel By The Sea. Open at all times to those of all faiths." Dan got out, came around and handed her out of the car. A tiny shock tingled her arm, the touch of his hand seeming more fiery than the heat of the brilliant sunshine that warmed her head and shoulders.

Puzzled, Ashly glanced up at him. "Are we going to church?"

Dan laughed. "No, but we'll look inside if you like. They say it's lovely."

At Ashly's smiling nod, he clasped her elbow and led her to the door.

The instant she stepped inside the cool, dim sanctuary, a sense of tranquility flowed through her that she hadn't known in months. Her gaze swept over pale blue walls, windows whose drawn blinds shut out the heat of the day; beige wooden pews with pale blue cushions. At the far end of the chapel stood a dark wooden pulpit, a mahogany organ and an altar table which held a gleaming gold cross, gold vases and candlesticks. A soft breeze stirred her hair, caressed her cheek, and Ashly glanced upward. Two ceiling fans slowly revolved, and green-shaded hurricane lamps glowed with an ethereal light.

Captivated by the sweet simplicity, soothed by the serenity of the sanctuary, Ashly closed her eyes in silent prayer. Sensing Dan standing at her side, she turned to look up at him. His face bore an expression of unbelievable tenderness that vanished so quickly that she wasn't certain she had really seen it.

He curved an arm about her shoulders and gave her a gentle hug. "Peace," he said softly.

Her eyes misted. Somehow he understood the turmoil seething deep within her and needed to say no more to show he cared. Together they ambled out into the warm spring sunshine.

His deep, pleasant voice turned solemn as he spoke his thoughts aloud. "Sometimes I think old William Wordsworth was right. The world *is* too much with us. I guess that's why I love my work—though some people don't think much of it." He threw her a sidelong smile. "If you're lucky enough to stumble on a place like this, you can hide away from all the everyday pressures, a sort of a self-renewal." He gestured toward a sun-dappled glade bounded by a low stone wall. "This old cemetery's been here for a hundred years. Not a bad place to be laid to rest."

Ashly bit her lip, tensed as he led her through the low wall. They strolled along the sandy paths of the graveyard reading inscriptions blurred by buffeting winds, sand, and water on the ancient, scarred stone markers.

Dan paused before a small granite stone. "Listen to this: 'John A. Bryant, born June 21, 1905, died March 21, 1910. Christ found him and took him home.'" Dan shook his head. "People sure didn't last long in those days."

Something inside Ashly's head snapped. Frightened, angry, she spun to face him, her eyes accusing. "You sound so heartless, so callous and unfeeling."

Dan's brows rose in astonishment. Gently he said, "Not so, Ashly. Realistic." Glancing about him, he threw out his hands in a helpless gesture. "There must be a dozen infants and children buried here. All I meant was that it's a damn shame their lives ended prematurely."

With a violent motion Ashly clapped her hands over her ears. "Stop! Oh, stop! I hate cemeteries! Why did you bring me here?"

In the same breath, she thought: *I'm being so unfair. I should have told Dan from the start that my husband was killed in a plane crash.* But she couldn't bear to talk about her husband without going to pieces, then, or now.

He reached out and touched her cheek. Softly he said, "I thought you'd enjoy visiting a quiet, peaceful place—enjoy reading the old tombstones...." His voice was drowned out by the loud staccato drone of a helicopter overhead.

Ashly whirled away from him and ran across the white raked sands, past seagrape, palm, and cactus, toward the parking area. Even with her hands over her ears, her mind replayed the deafening roar, screaming sirens, and people shouting, crying for help, floundering in dark, freezing water. And as she relived the crash, guilt overwhelmed her. Guilt that she had not saved Werner. Guilt that so many had died and she had lived.

Dan broke into a run. As the sound of the helicopter faded away, he found Ashly seated in the MG, slumped over the dashboard, her head buried in her arms. He reached out, placed a hand on the back of her neck. A violent shudder shook her slender body. He slid a hand under her collar. Her skin felt cold to his touch. A terrible fear shot through him.

"Ashly, are you all right?"

When she made no reply, he cried out, "Oh, God, Ashly, speak to me!" He flung the door open and gathered her to him. Instantly, he recoiled in shock. Her body felt clammy and she was shaking all over. Gripping her tightly, he slid onto the seat and cradled her in his arms. His heart thudded with fear as he gazed down at her. Eyes closed, thick-fringed lashes brushing her cheeks, she lay motionless against his chest.

He pressed her head against his shoulder and with his free hand stroked the tightly knotted muscles in her neck and shoulders, then kneaded every vertebra, his strong, supple fingers soothing, healing, working up and down the length of her slender back. Frantic with worry, he said softly, "I'm not going to take a chance trying to help you. I'm going to drive you to a doctor." Just then, she stirred in his arms and he saw a faint rosy tinge stain her cheeks.

She sat up straight, her gaze vague and disoriented. Dazedly, she smoothed her hair. Turning to face Dan, she shook her head in despair. "Sorry, Dan. I couldn't get my breath and then I just panicked—"

Gazing at her with kindly concern, he said quietly, "Like the day we met on the beach, right?"

Wordlessly she nodded. If only she could explain so he'd understand. She took a deep breath. "My husband died in a plane crash a few months ago. I survived. I tried to save him—but I couldn't find him." She swallowed hard, forcing herself to go on. "The terror that I felt—sometimes it just sweeps over me—"

Dan placed his hands on her cheeks, gazing earnestly into her eyes. "I'm glad you finally told me. I didn't know. I didn't understand."

She twisted away from the gentle persuasion of his comforting hands, warm on her cheeks. How could she ever explain how it really felt to survive a crash that had killed her husband and more than one hundred people? How helpless and angry and frustrated she still felt?

"I can't talk about it Dan. I'm sorry." A pang of sadness knifed through her. Silent, unmoving, she perched on the seat like a fledgling poised for flight. She felt his body tense, his arms tighten about her waist.

In rough, yet not unkind tones, he said, "I've no idea how long you've been alone, but it looks to me as if you're clinging to your husband's memory as if your life depended on it. I know there's no use telling you to stop hurting yourself or to let go. He shook his head, smiling ruefully. "I've been there." His voice turned husky, soothing. "Give it time, Ashly. Only time can vanquish ghosts."

She looked at him in numbed silence. There was more to it than that, much more. Couldn't he accept the fact that she didn't want to talk about it? Panic closed her throat, choking her. If he said one more word, she'd jump from the car and run.

He plunged a hand inside his jeans pocket and withdrew it, his fingers curled into a loose fist. A pleased, secretive expression crossed his face. "For you," he said softly.

"For me! What is it?"

His lips curved in an enigmatic smile. "Look and see."

She made a great show of uncurling his tanned, sturdy fingers one by one. In the hollow of his palm, in polished perfection, lay her junonia shell.

She smiled up at him. "Oh, I'm so glad you found it! When I hold it in my hand I feel—," she broke off, about to say, "—that you are with me and nothing bad can happen." Instead, she said, "I feel so safe."

Impulsively, she kissed him full on the mouth. His lips, warm and wonderfully inviting, responded in a way that made her heart pound. She felt her cheeks flame as she saw the pleased, startled expression in his eyes. Swiftly she drew back from him, and a gleam of amusement flickered in their smoky depths, but all he said was, "You okay now?"

She nodded. "Okay!" True, she had recovered her composure, but what was not okay was that her memories of the days they had shared, his compelling, sensuous gaze, his tantalizing lips, his tender caresses, would haunt her heart forever.

He nodded toward a break in the trees on the far side of the cemetery. "There's a path leading down to the beach. Come on—race you to the water. I'll give you a headstart." Grinning, he flung open the door, curved a hand under her bottom and gave her a gentle shove.

Ashly leaped from the car and broke into a run. Dan,

jogging close on her heels, couldn't pass her without scraping against the needle-sharp spines of prickly-pear cactus that bordered the path.

"Run!" he shouted in teasing tones. He reached out, grabbed a corner of the pink silk scarf that bound her hair and yanked, waving it like a banner over his head. Ashly shrieked in mock terror as her hair tumbled down her back, streaming on the wind.

Dan clasped Ashly's hand as they emerged from the shaded, winding path. The white sand beach was deserted except for two small boys building a sand castle and two young lovers, stretched out on a striped towel soaking up the sun. They kicked off their shoes, raced across the sand and splashed into the foam-embroidered waves. When she would have slowed, Dan gripped her hand more tightly. His free arm encircled her narrow waist as they dashed into the surf. A lightheartedness that she had never felt before swept through her. An incoming wave struck them and a chill tingled through her body from fingertips to toes.

They stood knee-deep in the bouyant, salty surf, watching the waves recede, holding hands and jumping over the low breakers that came crashing onto shore. The cool salt spray shot up into their faces and droplets of water glistened on their skin. Without warning a monstrous wave came rolling into shore, curling high over their heads, knocking them off their feet. Ashly shrieked in mock terror. Laughing, Dan pulled her against his chest, holding her tightly imprisoned within his strong, muscular arms. The incoming tide rolled them over and his legs locked with hers as they were swept toward shore.

Breathless, exhilarated, laughing, they regained their feet, drenched and dripping. Ashly clung to Dan, one arm about his neck, the other about his waist. Swiftly he slid an arm under her knees, curved the other around her back and, carrying her high above the breakers, strode from the water and set her gently down upon the shore. A wayward breeze caught them, raising gooseflesh on Ashly's gleaming wet skin.

Grinning, he sank down beside her. "This is the best way I know to 'dry out.'"

Ashly couldn't hide the fond look in her eyes. "I'm with you."

Dan scooped up a handful of sand and held it out to her. "I wish they were diamonds."

Ashly laughed. "You've already plied me with food and wine." She closed her eyes and gave herself over to reveling in the brilliance of the sunshine that bathed the seascape in a radiant light; the soothing sound of waves lapping upon the shore; the tangy fragrance of the salt air, but most of all she reveled in the sheer joy, the bliss of being with Dan, all the more poignant, because she would soon leave him.

As they lay stretched out on their backs, side by side, Dan told Ashly more about his work, and how he'd become so involved. As a small boy growing up on the island— an only child, lonely, he'd spent every minute exploring, discovering his world of nature. His eyes sparkled with enthusiasm. "I knew I could never know enough, never learn all there is to know." He took her hand in his, holding it tenderly. "So you see why I'm on a crusade to preserve the island, why I'm a sworn enemy of your brother-in-law. It's nothing personal, I'm sure he's a nice guy and under other circumstances, I'd like him. I just hate what he's doing."

With a reassuring smile, Ashly nodded. "I understand." And then she told him how she and her sister had grown up in a sedate suburb of Boston; how, after their parents' death, she had tried to keep Jessamine in college, but Jess, unwilling to burden Ashly further, found a job modeling. Lured by the bright lights and excitement, the promise of fame, Jess had tripped off to New York.

"She has this bloom about her, a fresh, natural beauty that made it all too easy to command a top salary," said Ashly ruefully. "All too easy to quit college."

Smiling into her eyes, Dan interrupted. "I grant you, Jessamine is beautiful, but as far as I can see, it's only skin-deep. Her sister is much more beautiful!"

Blushing, Ashly laughed. "You know what they say. 'Beauty is in the eye of the beholder!'" And then she told him how her parents had died in a boating accident and, orphaned young, how devoted she and Jessamine had become, were still; how she hated to be a burden on Jessamine and Ted. With these shared confidences, a deeper understanding, an empathy that she had never felt with anyone else, sprang up between them.

During the ride home, Ashly sat silent, reluctant to end the magical sense of euphoria that had enveloped them. She suppressed an ecstatic sigh. How marvelous it would be to share every moment of every day with Dan Kendall. It came to her with startling clarity that in sharing her fears with Dan they were halved; in sharing the good times, her joy was doubled. As if sensing her thoughts, he reached across and covered her hand with his, tightening in a companionable squeeze as their fingers entwined on the warm leather seat of the MG.

"Why so quiet, friend?"

She turned to smile at him. "Daydreaming."

A half-smile quirked at the corners of his mouth. "Better than nightmares, any time."

"Right. And the next time one sneaks up on me, I'll remember today." A wistful note entered her voice. "I'm going to miss Sanibel."

His light, bristly brows drew together in a scowl. "Forget it!"

"It's true, Dan. I *love* the island, the exotic trees and plants, the beauty and charm of the town, the people...."

"I mean, forget leaving," he said gruffly.

She shook her head, and a lump rose in her throat. "I was foolish to stay this long."

For a long moment he was silent, a thoughtful expression on his tanned, rugged features. At last he said, "There is a way you could stay."

DREAM OF LOVE

Her heart turned over. Her light blue eyes widened as she looked at him in silent question.

Quietly he said, "You could stay at my place."

Ashly shook her head. "Impossible."

As though she hadn't spoken, he went on. "There's not much room in the cabin. The otters are still there, and an owl, a cat and several dogs, but—"

Quickly Ashly interrupted. "It's not a question of room. I could be deliriously happy in a one-room cabin with—your wildlife friends." She ran the tip of her tongue over dry lips. "But I can't freeload, Dan." Privately she thought that sharing a cabin with Dan Kendall could shatter the resolve of a saint, let alone her own battered resolutions to keep free of any emotional involvements.

Unperturbed, he said, "Not to worry about freeloading. We can't hire anyone at the Center right now, but we desperately need help. You could volunteer. And I'd sure appreciate your help with my sick and injured animals. In return, I'll donate bed and board. Fair exchange?"

Ashly glanced at him skeptically. "Whose bed?"

The corners of his mouth twitched in amusement. "Your own bed, in a room of your own—unless you want to volunteer for night duty."

Ashly laughed. "Forget it."

Dan cocked an indignant eyebrow at her. "As a matter of fact, the cabin is reserved for my four-footed friends, fish and winged visitors, but I own a beach house nearby." He gave her a crooked grin. "I'll bunk in the cabin. You can have the beach house till you find a place to live and a paying job."

Ashly, staring at him thunderstruck, gave a vigorous shake of her head.

"Ashly, please don't give me an automatic reject. *Think* about it."

Distraught, she merely nodded, glad he couldn't know what she was thinking. It could be a long time before she found a paying job and a place to live until Palm Air took her back. On the other hand, her insurance check could come any day now. Ted had said if she invested the money she could carefully be financially independent. She sighed inwardly. The insurance check would make no difference. She wanted to work, loved working, loved meeting people. Working at the Center would be stimulating, exciting, challenging. Volunteering with Dan, where she could see him, hear him, touch him, would be like healing. Who else would hire someone who could have a panic attack or sink into a depression at any time, much less pay her enough to live on?

She should give him a flat out, "No," here and now. But the beach house was terribly tempting. Maybe living there alone, she'd find the peace and quiet she needed to get her life on track. But Dan would never be far away. Every minute of every hour she would be aware of his disturbing presence. Suppressing a sigh, she said, "No thanks, Dan. It wouldn't work."

In a husky voice he said, "Listen, Ashly, you'd be doing me a favor. I'm tired of talking to the walls." His mouth widened in an appealing grin. "I'm even tired of talking to myself!"

Ashly's silvery laughter rippled through the soft, dusky air. "I don't believe it!"

But Dan wasn't laughing. He looked terribly serious and when he spoke his voice rang with such conviction that her heart began to pound.

"You need me, Ashly. I ask for no commitments, agreed?"

"Absolutely no commitments, I heartily agree."

"I need you, Ashly, someone to share my thoughts, my hopes and dreams for the islands. And someone to help care for the sick and wounded, the abandoned creatures in my infirmary."

She turned her head away, unable to endure the hope she saw burning in the depths of his eyes. "I—I'll have to mull it over, Dan." Frantically she tried to find the right words to let him down gently.

Dan made no reply. Mile after mile they rode in silence,

each engrossed in thought. The MG was rolling through a long stretch of cool, green woodland dappled with early evening sunlight when Dan slowed and swung onto a two-lane track barely visible from the road. Whistling a cheerful tune, he guided the car past thick scrub, a stand of tall pines, cabbage palms, and live oaks bearded with clumps of blue-gray Spanish moss.

Quietly Ashly asked, "Where are we going?"

"Home."

"Home! To your place?"

"Right."

Blood drummed in her ears. "I thought we agreed I'd mull it over."

"Right," he said, in high good humor. "Now you've had time to mull it over. So it's settled."

Ashly's mouth fell open. "But I never agreed—"

"Silence lends consent." He appeared enormously pleased with himself.

When she opened her mouth to protest, Dan pressed a finger against her lips. "Quiet! You'll wake the patients!" He slowed the car to a stop before a rustic log cabin nestled under a cluster of sabal palms and announced cheerfully, "Here we are, home!"

Leaning forward to see through the trees, Ashly gasped. She had expected to see a small, one-room cabin. This was twice the size she'd envisioned, with a spacious wing in back, glassed-in windows, and a massive stone chimney that promised cozy, roaring fires on damp winter days.

"This must be the top-of-the-line luxury model," she breathed, taken aback.

"Hardly, although it does have four rooms. One is an office, two rooms serve as an infirmary for itinerant wildlife, and," he smiled wryly, "I bed down in another when I stay over with a sick friend. There's a small kitchen and bath in back."

Ashly's gaze strayed to a wire fence stretched along a row of wooden posts. "What's the fenced-in area?"

"That's where we dug the loggerhead nests before we

set up a hatchery farther down the beach. Now our patients use it. They can go outdoors and be protected from predators."

Ashly gazed at him in amazement. Never had she met a man so masculine, so virile, who could also be so gentle and generous of heart. Like a latterday Pied Piper, he charmed her, lured her to follow after him. A lure she knew she must resist.

Dan drove on through the thick woodland. Once Ashly glimpsed a flash of shimmering aquamarine water, but saw no sign of a house. "Good heavens, your place is certainly well hidden!"

"I enjoy my privacy," he replied smiling. He drove up a curving shell driveway and drew to a stop in a circular turnaround. "Here we are!"

Ashly stared, blinked and stared again, long and hard. If she had been taken aback at the sight of Dan's cabin, she was totally nonplussed at the sight of his beach house.

Chapter 9

Ashly sat mesmerized, her gaze riveted on the house. Set well back from the beach, almost hidden among soaring pines, live oaks and clumps of cabbage palms, stood a multi-level house of weathered brown cedar perched on concrete stilts. Laurel, crimson hibiscus, and flowering shrubs added splashes of color to an emerald green lawn. A neat wooden sign set in the ground read KENDALL'S EDEN.

"Well?" Dan asked, a roguish glint sparkling in his eyes. "Are you going to get out?"

Ashly nodded, but her arms and legs refused to move. Dan opened the car door and taking a hand, pulled her to her feet. Speechless, she stood entranced. The soft brown cedar walls blended with the woodland setting, hiding the house from view of passersby on the beach. Beyond the bleached white shore stretched the sparkling cobalt waters of the Gulf.

Dan's hand tightened around hers. "Let's move inside."

Wonderingly, Ashly looked up into his face. His eyes crinkled at the corners, his lips quirked with suppressed laughter at her astonished reaction, no doubt. She blushed.

"Not a standard beach house. You might have warned me."

Dan gave a derisive hoot. "Never judge a snail by its shell."

"Some shell!"

He shrugged, glancing nonchalantly at the house. "It's not that important. It's like buying a new car, a new coat, a new anything. After it's been around awhile, you don't really see it." Shoving his hands in his jeans pockets, he sauntered on, nodding toward a huge concrete block next to the stilts. "Game room, sauna, and garage. Not much to see there."

He led her up an outside wooden staircase. On the landing, he flung open a door and ushered her inside an entry hall with a mirrored wall and stained glass windows whose brilliant blues, yellows, and green shone on the white tiled floor.

Through an archway, Ashly glimpsed a sunken living room with a cathedral ceiling that glowed under concealed lights. Dan flipped on a wall switch and soft, romantic music flowed around them like an embrace. He touched a button beside the mirrored wall in the foyer and Ashly stifled a gasp as two panels parted, opening onto an elevator with plush cream carpeting.

"We'll start at the top." Dan looked at her, his lips curved in a teasing grin. "That's one of my precepts, starting at the top."

"Starting at the top must be terribly risky. After all, the only way to go is down. Did you by any chance win the lottery?"

"Money is a curse I was born with," Dan said cheerfully. "You see, my ancestors were among the first settlers on the island, part of a fleet of shrimpers off the Keys. They came to Sanibel on vacation and built the cabin as a sort of retreat."

Ashly's brows rose in surprise. "According to Ted's map, this is the Richardson Tract. He was told no one is allowed to build here. How come *you* wrangled a permit?"

Color seeped up Dan's chiseled features into his hairline. With good-humored frankness, he said, "I'm a privileged character. The late Mister Richardson happened to be my grandfather. He invested in huge tracts of land and I inherited the property. I then deeded the tract to the city for a wildlife preserve, except for this plot for my own use."

"I see," said Ashly softly. She saw as well a thinking, caring man who was making Sanibel a better place for having lived here. The elevator glided to a stop. The doors slid open and they stepped out onto thick white carpeting.

Dan gestured toward an open doorway. "My private suite. I call it the Captain's Quarters because there's a crow's nest outside with a fantastic view for miles around."

Ashly paused in the doorway, her dazzled gaze sweeping over a spacious airy room decorated in shades of hot pink, moss green and starched white, with bamboo armchairs, a king-size bed, and pots of flowering pink dogwood.

"It's lovely," Ashly exclaimed. A bubble of laughter rose in her throat. If only Ted could see this beach bum's pad! Suddenly she became aware of Dan's quizzical gaze upon her. As if he'd read her thoughts, the corners of his mouth quirked with suppressed laughter.

He reached down and took her hand in his. "Come along, dumplin'. I'll show you the view from the Crow's Nest." Gently he propelled her toward a sliding glass wall. They stepped onto a wide, wooden balcony and stood as though transfixed, his arm about her shoulders, gazing out over the Gulf. Ashly's breath caught in her throat. Sky and Gulf merged in a vast azure tapestry streaked with ribbons of pale peach and gold flowing above silver-tipped crests of the ultramarine waters.

Her gaze traveled slowly across bleached sands to the velvety green oasis beyond the house where an oval pool was set like a sparkling turquoise stone in a white pebbled deck. Strewn about the pool were yellow wrought iron tables and chairs under the shade of swaying, fan-shaped palms.

Enthralled, Ashly said, "It's unreal! Like a movie set!"

His warm, penetrating gaze locked with hers for an endless moment. "*You* are unreal! Lovelier than any star shining on earth, sea, or—"

Grinning, she reached up and pressed her fingers against his lips. "*You* are unreal, Dan Kendall!" She longed to believe him, but did not dare. For the hundredth time, she reminded herself that she wanted no emotional entanglements to complicate her life. Before he could say anything further, she said softly, "Show me the rest of the house, Dan." Quickly she turned and strode toward the elevator.

As they rode down, she saw him watching her, an amused glint in his eyes, but he said no more until they emerged on the floor below. Casually he said, "There are three bedrooms on this level. Take whichever one you like."

Though the first two rooms were light, airy and attractively furnished, the minute Ashly entered the third room, she fell in love with it. Directly below Dan's quarters, overlooking the Gulf, a wall of windows opened onto a balcony where an ancient Australian pine stood guard. Filmy blue chiffon draperies framed the windows, and above the satin-quilted bed and tufted headboard, a blue, silk canopy was gathered into a gilt crown. She spun to face Dan, her eyes shining with pleasure.

"This is the most heavenly room I've ever seen. I'd feel like the grandest tigress in the jungle, sleeping here."

He grinned down at her. "It's yours. Reserved for the sleeping tigress."

Tucking her arm in his, he led her onto the balcony and down a wooden staircase that gave onto a wide sundeck running the length of the house. Through sliding glass doors, they entered a spacious country kitchen. Milk-glass globes hanging from a beamed ceiling shed their soft glow over dark oak cabinets, beige-tiled counters, and every appliance anyone could want. Nonplussed, Ashly stared about her. But what struck her most was the air of emptiness that pervaded the room. She let out her breath slowly.

"This is beautiful, Dan—like a page in a decorator magazine—almost too pretty to use."

His expression turned somber. "It isn't used. Never has been. I built this house for my wife—to keep up her spirits, to give her something to look forward to when she came home from the hospital. She never came home."

Ashly felt a sudden ache in her throat. She longed to put her arms around him, to comfort him. Softly, she said, "I'm sorry."

With a strained smile, he quickly changed the subject. "I usually cook in the cabin." As though struck with an idea, he brightened. "Maybe you'd like to cook something here—rustle up an omelet?"

Suddenly she sensed a loneliness about him, a yearning she'd not seen before. She smiled up at him. "I'd love to."

He threw out his hands in a helpless gesture. "The cupboard's bare, but I'll stop at Bailey's and pick up some food."

They sauntered through the dining room across a gleaming parquet floor, past a glass-topped table and bamboo armchairs with plump white cushions set on a pastel dhurrie rug. Overhead a chandelier with fluted shades shaped like lion's paws shed a soft radiance.

The glass-walled living room offered a magnificent view of the Gulf. Ashly's gaze swept over a sea of plush, rust-colored carpet, a curved beige velvet couch strewn with pillows and a huge fieldstone fireplace with an impressive ship's clock on the mantel. She breathed an ecstatic sigh. The elegant house, soft lights, and romantic music all created a perfect setting.

Too perfect, she thought—like a movie set soon to be dismantled and stored away. It came to her then what was wrong with the place. It lacked a human touch, a woman's touch. Suddenly she longed to live here, to bring love, warmth, and laughter, to bring this house to life. Instantly, she chided herself. She was far from ready for love.

They rode the elevator to the ground floor and as Dan

flung open the door into the garage, Ashly let out an incredulous gasp. Standing in solitary splendor in the three-car garage stood a gleaming silver-gray sedan with whitewall tires and a kneeling lady on the radiator cap.

She tuned to Dan. "A Rolls-Royce!"

He nodded. "A Silver Cloud, built in the fifties."

"How come you never drive it?"

He waved a hand in casual dismissal. "I don't really need it. Bought it to help out a friend who needed quick cash."

Ashly felt a warm rush of affection toward this generous, caring man. Smiling, she said, "Your forte seems to be rescuing creatures in distress and keeping them—"

Dan interrupted, eyeing her with mock severity. "Hold it. I never keep them captive. I always release them when they're ready to go."

Was he trying to tell her something, with his talk of letting go? No matter. Without realizing it, she'd made up her mind. She knew absolutely that she should not stay at Kendall's Eden. But she lacked the strength to resist. She would stay only until she could fly again for Palm Air. The prospect filled her with mingled anticipation and apprehension.

They climbed in the MG and as Rex guided the car down the driveway, Ashly said, "Back to Jessamine's, right?"

"Right." His lips curved in a cheerful grin. "To pick up your gear."

Ashly laughed. "You can't be serious."

His voice held a note of finality. "I was never more serious in my life."

She looked at him, astonished. "I can't walk out cold. Can't do that to Jessamine. Besides, Ted isn't home. I can't leave without thanking him for all he's done for me."

His jaw tightened in a stubborn, bull-headed way that signaled trouble. "Ashly, you're not making sense. Not three hours ago you told me it was time to cut out."

With an effort she kept her voice calm and reasonable. "Well, yes, but there's no need to rush."

Dan looked at her long and hard. Emphatically he said, "The time to leave is now. If you don't, when Ted comes home he'll use his gentle persuasion to pressure you and it will be even harder to leave."

She wanted to tell him he was wrong, but they both knew better. Avoiding his gaze, she said nothing.

He braked the car at the end of the narrow lane and turned to face her. Gently he said, "Once you make up your mind, it's best to follow through. More ground is lost in this world by inaction than by the doing of deeds. It's not the things you do in life that you regret, it's the things you *don't* do! Believe me, I know." Gunning the motor, he swung onto the San-Cap Road.

Whether his gentle lecture referred to the apathy of the public in conserving the environment, or to her dragging her heels, she couldn't tell. She sat quietly, hands clenched in her lap, feeling nervous and upset. How could she simply walk out on Jessamine? Jess would be devastated that she was leaving, and worse, that she was going to live in Dan Kendall's house. There had to be another way. When they arrived at Jessamine's, she would simply refuse to leave.

As if he'd sensed her rebellion, the moment Jessamine opened the door, Dan made a polite bow and in his most charming voice, with his most engaging smile, said, "We're here to collect Ashly's things, Jessamine. She's moving to Kendall's Eden."

Jessamine's brows flew up and staring at Ashly in disbelief, she said, "Ashly, you're not serious!"

In tones that brooked no argument, Ashly said, "Jessamine, I'm going to be a volunteer at the Nature Center. In return Dan has offered me a place to stay."

Eyes wide with astonishment, Jessamine gazed at Ashly. "Ashly Swann, I think you've flipped."

Chapter 10

Open-mouthed, Ashly stared at Jessamine, feeling an unexpected surge of remorse at abandoning her sister.

"Jess, I'm sorry to walk out on you and Ted. You've been so wonderful to me, but—"

Jessamine looked at Dan and Ashly. "Don't be sorry. I understand."

"I'm sure Ted won't."

"Well, he might not," Jessamine continued. "He told me again just this morning how much he enjoys having you with us. Ted wants you to stay as long as you like. We'll take care of you forever! I tried to tell him that forever is a bit much, but—"

Ashly quailed inside. *Forever!* She felt the color drain from her face. Dan was right. She had to make the break. She crossed to Jessamine and gripped her shoulders. "Please explain to Ted that you *have* done everything— more than anyone could ask, but I need to be on my own. I can't keep imposing on you."

Jessamine wrapped her arms around Ashly, hugging her tightly. "Imposing? Never. You're family. But—" She cast a dubious look at Dan and lowered her voice so only Ashly could hear. "He's not."

"Jess, please listen to me. I'm *earning* my way, volunteering at the Center. And, in exchange for room and board, I'll help Dan care for his animals at his cabin. I'll have a room of my own."

Doubt contorted Jessamine's perfect features. "In a cabin? Some tumble-down shack? Ashly, darling, we want only the best for you. A city girl like you isn't going to be happy living like an outcast in the woods with a bunch of animals."

"I'm not living in the cabin," Ashly said. "Dan will live there. I'm staying in his beach house."

"Does it have *indoor* plumbing?" Jessamine asked worriedly.

Ashly smiled. "Yes, Jess, it has indoor plumbing."

Jessamine grasped both Ashly's hands and drew her down on the couch. "Darling, why not wait till Ted comes home. You can make him understand.

"No, Jess," she said firmly. "Ted doesn't have to be happy for me. Just tell him I'll be back to thank him for everything."

"But Ashly—"

Smoothly, Dan interrupted, "Ashly, get your things. We're leaving *now!*"

Jessamine gazed at him for a long, silent moment. Turning back to Ashly, she put her arms around her and gave her a hug. "Ted and I want only what is best for you."

Softly Ashly said, "I know, Jess, but it's *my* life we're talking about, and *my* decision. This is a perfect solution for me. And if you need me when the baby comes, I'll be right here." She stood up. "I'll go pack my things."

Jessamine followed her from the room, her warm voice floating down the hall. "If you're sure this is what you want, then I'm all for it. But remember, our door is always open. All we want is for you to be happy."

"Jess," came Ashly's voice, firm and clear. "I'm going to be happy."

Dan let out a long, relieved sigh.

Driving back to the beach house along the smooth blacktop road, Dan reached out and squeezed Ashly's hand. "Don't worry, Ashly, you've done the right thing."

Her heart turned over. He sounded so sincere, genuinely concerned. His kindness tugged at some tender place inside her where she had thought there was nothing but scar tissue. Tears stung her eyelids as she fixed her gaze on the fiery sun slipping below the glassy-smooth waters of the Gulf. How could she be so vulnerable? Her hand trembled under Dan's warm, strong clasp.

She couldn't stay with Jess and Ted forever. She would have to make a new life for herself sometime. Dan's offer was a heaven-sent chance. He was good for her; she needed him. Sternly she told herself that the fact that she wanted to be with him more than anyone else in the world had nothing to do with her decision. Nothing at all. Without volition, her fingers curled around his hand in a companionable squeeze.

As if sensing her distress, Dan said, "We'll stop by the house, change into presentable clothes, then we'll have dinner at the Bubble Room—to celebrate your declaration of independence."

She cast him a sidelong glance to see if he was teasing her, but his expression was solemn, with no hint of laughter.

"Recognize anyone?" Dan asked, leaning across the table toward Ashly.

They were seated in a booth at the Bubble Room, in one of several low-ceilinged rooms decorated with memorabilia from the Thirties, Forties, and Fifties. Ashly was staring entranced at a toy train running on a track hung from the ceiling. The engine's bell dinged above the sound of nostalgic songs playing in the background.

Now aware of Dan's intense gaze upon her, she smiled back at him. "Sorry, I was wool-gathering."

Dan grinned. "I asked if you recognized anyone. Not the diners, the photos."

Ashly's gaze roved about the walls papered with photos of movie stars popular in bygone days. She shook her head, her fall of golden hair brushing her cheeks. "Only Marilyn Monroe and Bogie—I've seen them in old movies. But I hear someone—Perry Como?—lamenting that he's a prisoner of love."

Dan's dark, glowing eyes bored into hers with an intensity that took her breath away. Softly he said, *"I'm* a prisoner of love!"

Ashly's heart began to pound. These were words she longed to hear, but she dared not listen. To cover her confusion, she smiled, then staring at Dan, her smile widened. "Dan, your face is turning green."

Feigning alarm, he ran his hand across his forehead, down his cheek, across his smoothly shaven jaw. "Must be the weather—unseasonably warm. I'm molting."

Laughing, Ashly nodded toward a string of colorful bubble lamps strung around the window. "I hope it's only a reflection."

Solemnly, Dan asked, "Do you think a green pallor becomes me?"

Ashly nodded. "You're quite a colorful character, Mister Kendall."

With an air of injured pride, he threw out his arms and stared down at his boldly striped blue, red, green, and yellow silk shirt. "Who, me?"

Ashly grinned. "I didn't mean your clothes."

Nevertheless, he had dressed to the hilt in a silk knit shirt and perfectly tailored chino slacks. Had he dressed his best to please her? She drew a deep breath and caught the scent of his aftershave lotion. The spicy, sensuous aroma made her senses reel.

She had dressed to please him, in a full turquoise skirt and sunshine-colored blouse. A wide kelly green leather belt cinched her narrow waist. On her feet she wore high-heeled, multi-colored sandals.

His eyes softened. His admiring gaze caressed her face. "You look especially enchanting tonight."

Her eyes meeting his held a warm, intimate expression. Then realizing her glance betrayed more than she wanted him to see, she looked quickly down at the "song titled" menu.

Dan gave their order to a "Bubble Scout" waitress clad in khaki shorts and shirt. When she returned with their dinner, Ashly eyed the brown-paper-wrapped entree on Dan's plate curiously. "What's your song title?"

"Eddy Fisherman's Catch of the Day. Grouper baked in a paper bag." A roguish look glistened in his eyes. "But I've already caught the catch of the day."

She blushed with pleasure and her heart began to hammer. Did he too, feel an exciting new warmth and intimacy flowing between them? He speared a morsel of fish on his fork and held it out to her. "Taste?"

She leaned toward him and slid the delicately flavored fish into her mouth, rolling her eyes heavenward. "Fantastic!"

Still watching her, Dan asked, "What's yours?"

"Bing and Bob Seafood Shiskabob Broiled on a Skewer. Have a scallop." She held the skewer toward him and he slid one off with his fork.

As he munched the scallop, Ashly said, "That's how I feel—like a fishkabob, broiled on a skewer. As if you'd speared me like a fish in the ocean and brought me in to cook over a hot grill."

Dan burst out laughing and lifting his wineglass, said, "A toast to the fish that almost got away!"

Joining in his laughter, Ashly touched her glass to his. All through their meal, Ashly couldn't keep her eyes from Dan. And every time she looked up, he was watching her, a bemused smile curving his lips.

When they had finished dinner, Ashly leaned back against the padded leather booth. She felt completely relaxed, warm and safe, utterly happy. Her languorous mood was interrupted by the waitress pushing a dessert cart laden with pastries: delectable-looking tortes, cakes and pies, and cherry and blueberry tarts.

Ashly groaned. "I couldn't eat another bite."

"You haven't lived till you've tasted Katie's cake. Katie and Jamie own the place, and this is her original creation."

At his nod, the waitress set before her a plate bearing a high, spongy yellow confection heaped with fluffy white frosting and slivered almonds. After devouring a small bite, Ashly said, "It's pure heaven—light as angel's wings." When she had finished the last crumb, she rested her head against the back of the booth, her eyes half closed in dreamy contentment.

Through lowered lids, she saw the hostess leading a party of four women to a vacant table less than six feet away. The next instant her body went rigid. She felt as if she were turning to stone. Small golden palm trees glinted on the lapels of the women's dark green jackets. Ashly paled. They couldn't be, but they were: Flight attendants from her class at Palm Air Academy. She squared her shoulders, bracing herself, her fingers clutching her wineglass.

Dan leaned toward her, alarm mirrored in his eyes. "Ashly, what's wrong?"

She sat as though transfixed, her eyes riveted on the girls crowding around the table. Any second one of them would recognize her. There would be excited exclamations of joy at seeing her alive and well, murmurs of sympathy over the loss of her husband, and endless question. She couldn't endure it if they asked what happened, listened in fascinated horror to every detail of the crash that could have happened to them, could still happen. Or they would tell her how lucky she was to be alive, when she herself never stopped wondering why such a disaster had to happen at all. She couldn't bear it.

She glanced frantically around her. There was nowhere

to run, no place to hide. She was trapped in the booth. She shrank back into the corner, turned her face to the wall and shut her eyes tight. If she could avoid eye contact, maybe they wouldn't notice her. If they saw her, maybe no one would recognize her. After all they would never expect to see her here.

Dan reached across the table and took her cold, damp hands in his strong grip. In commanding tones he said, "Ashly, tell me what's wrong!"

She sat frozen, unable to speak. She heard a trill of laughter. Heard chairs scraping and a high-pitched voice complaining, "—can't stand the air conditioning blowing on me!" Then the hostess's low, accommodating tones offering another table and voices receding as the women trooped into another room.

Totally unnerved, grateful for the booth and its measure of privacy, Ashly let out her breath slowly. Aware of Dan's intense gaze upon her, she raised her eyes to meet his. He was looking at her with a searching expression, still holding her hands in his, awaiting some explanation.

The silence lengthened between them, taut as an elastic band. *Don't ask me,* she prayed. *All I want is to forget.* The words pounded in her ears, her mind, her heart.

Dan released her hands and leaned back in the booth, a set, closed expression on his face. Unable to stand his silence, Ashly ran the tip of her tongue over dry lips.

"I know those women—they're Palm Air flight attendants." She swallowed hard. "I was a flight attendant with Palm Air before—" she paused, unable to go on.

Dan's brows rose, "Before?"

The words burst from her lips. "Before the Palm Air crash last December."

She saw shocked dismay reflected in his eyes. "Was that the plane you were on?"

Mutely she nodded.

He leaned toward her, looking stunned and incredulous at the same time. "Good lord, how did you get out of it alive?"

In flat, choked tones, she said, "I don't want to talk about it. That's why I didn't want them to see me." Her throat closed. She felt she couldn't draw another breath. She clenched her hands in her lap and stared directly into his eyes with a defiant expression that commanded him to silence.

His eyes filled with sympathy, with wanting. Wanting to understand, wanting to comfort her. She caught her lip between her teeth to keep from crying out to him to stop looking at her that way.

His voice, low and warm, reached out to her. "Want to tell *me* about it?"

Frowning, Ashly shook her head.

Staring back at her, Dan gave a long sigh of defeat.

The warm intimacy that had sprung up between them dissolved like smoke in a brisk wind. She could almost feel him retreating from her.

With an air of finality, he placed both hands flat on the table and rose to his feet. "Let's go."

They wove their way toward the door, through the room where the Palm Air attendants were seated. Ashly noticed that Dan went out of his way to lead her down the far side of the room away from their table, and kept close to her side, as if to shield her from view. She looked up at him with a small, appreciative half-smile, but he was intent on extracting his credit card from his billfold.

They drove home in a silence that weighed more heavily than the hot, humid air that pressed around them. She knew that Dan felt rebuffed because she had refused to confide in him, refused any comfort he might offer. But she knew too, that with any show of sympathy, her defenses would crumble like a sand castle washing out to sea. She didn't know how to explain, how to convince him that she desperately needed to build her own strength, to be her own person before she could live again.

As Dan guided the MG up the dark driveway, the headlights' gleam spotlighted crimson hibiscus and velvet green lawns surrounding the house. At the sight of the weathered brown house in its peaceful woodland setting, Ashly's anxiety lessened. Dan cut the motor. She opened the door and slid out, then stood waiting while he found his keys and unlocked the door on the ground floor.

"I'll see you to your room," he said amiably.

She nodded, sighing inwardly, hoping he didn't intend to spend a few moments with her to comfort and reassure her.

They rode the elevator in awkward silence and, as if by common consent, clung to a fragile truce. The warmth of his body so close to hers, the seductive scent of his aftershave, assaulted her senses. She started to tell him she had recovered her composure, that she wanted to be alone, but she hated to wound him further. Though goodness knows, she told herself, the man has the ego of a lion.

She felt so tense that his every move took on an exaggerated importance. For no reason she found herself holding her breath as he stepped from the elevator, flicked on a light, then stood aside, waiting for her to precede him to her room.

In the doorway he touched a switch and the room sprang to life. Purposefully he crossed to the windows and drew the sheer blue draperies. A small stab of alarm ran up her spine. Without speaking, he strode to the thermostat. Watching his broad, muscular shoulders rippling under his shirt, she wondered what unleashed power, what depths of passion lay buried beneath that laid-back exterior. How would it feel to be the one who aroused this sleeping lion? But she mustn't indulge in such fantasies. She retreated to the side of the bed nearest the door. Idly she turned on a glass shell-filled lamp on the nightstand then stood quietly waiting, her gaze fixed on a gold-framed portrait of Dan smiling under the soft lamplight.

He wheeled to face her. Softly, he said, "You'll probably want to leave the air conditioning on all night to keep down the humidity."

She nodded.

"Eighty degrees?"

"Fine," she said crisply. He made her nervous, prowling about her room and she wished he'd go. But she didn't know what to say to a good Samaritan who had taken her in when she had nowhere else to go, and after all, this was *his* house.

He crossed to the far side of the king-size bed, reached behind the pillow and peeled back a corner of the pale blue quilted spread. "Grab a corner."

Ashly's mouth grew dry and she felt her pulse pounding in her temples. If he had in mind what she thought he had ... Together they folded down the spread. Dan reached under the pillow and drew back the blanket and sheet, exposing a pristine triangle of creamy satin sheet. Grinning, he flung out an inviting arm. "Be my guest."

Without knowing she was going to, she said quietly, "You're not planning to sleep here, are you?"

His blond, crescent brows lifted. Never taking his eyes from hers, he strode around the bed to where she stood. Curving a finger under her chin, he tilted her face up to his. "*Sleeping* in your bed was the furthest thing from my mind."

Ashly's senses whirled. Had he, or had he not, stressed the word "sleeping?"

Amusement glistened in his eyes. "I've more pressing things to do—like bedding down the animals for the night." Softly he said, "Sweet dreams, tigress." He strode through the doorway and closed the door firmly after him.

Chapter 11

During the days that followed, as if by tacit consent, Ashly and Dan carefully avoided the subject of conservation versus development of the island. Beneath the smooth surface of their days, the issue lay like a land mine which neither wanted to detonate. But a more immediate worry pressed on Ashly's mind.

When she moved to Kendall's Eden, she had promised herself she wouldn't indulge in romantic fantasies. Forewarned was forearmed. She only imagined she was falling in love with Dan Kendall. Naturally, she was attracted to him, but that's all it was. Now, despite all her resolves, she knew she was wrong. Only when she was with him did she feel truly alive. All she wanted was to be with him, day and night. Now she wondered how she could have deluded herself into thinking they could be simply good friends and companions? How could she have let her emotions rule her, when she had sworn never again to be so vulnerable? And worse, with a man vigorously at odds with her own family? Too late, she had realized they were becoming much too fond of each other. There lay the danger. Resolutely, she pushed the troublesome thoughts far back in her mind and plunged deep into work in the Center's native plant nursery.

When Ashly and Dan weren't busy with projects at the Center, they visited the picturesque old lighthouse at Point Ybel, or rode quaint, open-air, trolley busses the length of their green and orange routes. Occasionally they would go for a spin in the MG, rolling down the deserted shore road, laughing, singing at the tops of their lungs.

Or they biked along trails dappled with sunlight and shade, orange pennants fluttering in the sultry heat. Frequently they strolled the beach in the early morning or late afternoon, probing the fine white sand with shelling sticks, sharing their delight in discovering a perfectly formed angel wing or a lustrous pink-and-ivory whorled whelk.

It seemed that nothing would happen to change the even tenor of their days until the day in June that Jessamine and Ted's baby arrived six weeks early. To make matters worse, it was a scrawny, five-pound-one-ounce female with splotchy, red wrinkled skin and a tiny squinched-up face. A thatch of black hair sprouted from an oddly misshapen head. Though Ashly knew the elongated shape of her head was caused by the use of forceps during delivery and would soon right itself, tears dimmed her eyes as she gazed at the tiny infant through the hospital nursery window. So much for Jessamine's hope of a strapping son in Ted's image. If only she had been a plump, cherubic infant, Ted, who had waited out Jess's pregnancy in silent, stoic skepticism, might more easily have accepted her. He had taken one look at her and turned away. Jessamine loved the infant on sight and had declared her to be the most beautiful child ever born. She named her Ivy Rose.

One week later, Ashly stood looking lovingly down at Ivy Rose in her pink bassinet in her nursery at home. Ted hovered at the baby's side, staring down at her. He shook his head in mingled awe and disbelief. "Have you *ever* seen such a helpless female?" He picked her up and held her close to his chest, cradling her in one arm. With his free hand, he covered her tiny body in a protective gesture. Gazing down at the sleeping infant, he shook his head in wonder. "She's some little stranger!"

Ashly saw a look of compassion flash across Ted's face and quickly disappear. A pang of sympathy swept through her. Obviously, he knew, if Jessamine did not, that his infant was a tiny "plain Jane." He reached out a finger, chucking her under the chin. In a strong, staunch whisper he said, "Don't you worry, Ivy Rose. Your daddy will take care of you."

Ashly suppressed a grin. Later, she told Dan in jubilant tones, "Ted has a female who really needs him to take care of her. I guess I'm off the hook at last."

Whenever she had a free hour or two, Ashly would visit Jessamine and Ivy Rose. As the hot, humid August days passed, time and again, she put off leaving Sanibel because she hated to go. She loved caring for the baby, whose infant charms took her mind off Dan, let her forget for a few precious hours that the good times she and Dan shared would soon end. And then, one golden September day, to her astonishment, Dan said, "Mind if I go along?" Grinning, he added, "I have to see this miracle child."

Ashly felt a sudden lifting of her heart. "Glad to have you aboard."

"What about Ted? Will he be glad, too?"

Ashly nodded. "There's nothing Ted and Jess like better than showing off Ivy Rose."

When they arrived, Jessamine greeted Dan as though there had never been hard feelings between them. Blushing, she went on, "I must confess, both Ted and I agree you've been good for Ashly."

"I can't take credit. Her work at the Nature Center has occupied her time," he said, following her out to the lanai. Ted, seated in a bamboo armchair, held Ivy Rose in the crook of his arm. Mouth open wide as a baby bird, she allowed her father to spoon cereal into it. He greeted Ashly and Dan with a welcoming smile. "Say hello, Rosie." He gave the infant a gentle, loving poke. Rosie uttered a delighted babble of sounds clearly pleasing to herself and Ted. Ashly stood transfixed, watching Ted beam down on his daughter. An angel unaware, she had totally captured his heart and mind.

Dan gazed down at her as though mesmerized. At last he said, "She is the most beautiful baby I've ever seen."

Ted did a doubletake. "My thoughts exactly." He smiled at Dan. Dan smiled back.

Tentatively, Dan said, "We missed you at the zoning meeting last Friday."

Ted gave an abstracted nod. "I expect Sundance Resorts held up their end without me."

"Actually, we reached a compromise."

Intent on feeding Ivy Rose, Ted merely nodded. "I heard. After we complete our current project, we agreed to build no more condos on Sanibel in exchange for one location on the far side of Captiva."

Dan made no reply. Ashly knew he had no wish to start an argument. Silently, she marveled that to Ted, the importance of Sundance Resorts clearly paled in comparison to basking in the radiance of his baby daughter.

During the days that followed, Dan, apparently charmed by the infant, went to see her with Ashly whenever he could get away.

Time and again, when Ashly held her, Dan would look down at Ivy Rose with a soft, tender smile, then catch Ashly's eye. But all he ever said was, "For the first time in my life, I envy Ted LeBeau." Ashly's eyes misted, but there was nothing she could do. How could a woman who couldn't control her own life, be responsible for a tiny, helpless infant?

One mild, sun-drenched day when Ashly was rocking Ivy Rose, she became aware that the baby's opaque eyes had lightened to the gentian blue of Jessamine's. Her clear gaze seemed to focus on the faces that gazed so lovingly down on her, and her dainty pink mouth seemed to smile at everyone. More astonishing, whenever she cried, the only person who could quiet her was Ted.

Ivy Rose's arms and legs had rounded out and her pale skin glowed with a soft, silken sheen. Her head had assumed a beautiful round shape and her features had begun to form, giving her face an enchanting piquancy that was irresistible. The scrawny infant duckling was turning into a swan. And when Jessamine exclaimed again and again, "Isn't she the most beautiful child you've ever seen?" Ashly would say with heartfelt sincerity, "The most beautiful child in the world."

As the days flew by, Jessamine and Ted radiated a joy that enveloped everyone around them in its glow. Though Ashly rejoiced in their happiness, each time she and Dan left them, the static quality of their own existence knifed through her. How she longed for the warmth and closeness that united the little family they had just left. Instantly, she chided herself. She couldn't complain.

Yet, much as she loved working at the Nature Center, the future loomed bleakly before her like a vast chasm in which she was doomed to fall endlessly, never to land. Though her nightmares and anxiety attacks had subsided, they still haunted her. Her counselor had warned her that they could go on for years, that survival was an ongoing process, that she went into the crash one person and came out another. She wished she knew who that person was.

That night when Dan went to the cabin to bed down the animals, she called Jessamine on the phone. After several minutes of chatting about Ivy Rose, Ashly took a deep breath and said, "I had a special reason for calling."

Cheerfully, Jessamine said, "You sound serious . . ."

"I am serious. I'm leaving Sanibel."

"Oh, Ashly, no!" Jessamine wailed. "I was so afraid this would happen. I knew that staying with Dan wouldn't work out."

Ashly swallowed hard, forcing the words. "It isn't that things aren't working out. It's just time to leave."

"Darling, you *can't* leave! Where will you go? What will you do?"

"I'll be fine. Don't worry."

"Listen, Ashly. You move straight back here. Stay with us until you're reinstated with Palm Air."

In the background, she heard Ted chime in. "Tell her she's always welcome." She heard the baby gurgle, and Ted laughing. Her heart gave a painful twist. She would miss Rosie like blazes.

Jessamine giggled. "Ted's making funny faces at the baby, tickling her under the chin. Can you hear her?"

"I hear her," said Ashly softly. A giant hand seemed to squeeze her heart. Ted had finally found someone to whom he could be all things. It struck her then with blinding clarity that she had no place here either. No one needed her now.

Jessamine went on, her voice pleading, insistent. "Ashly, please stay with us. Your room is ready and waiting for you, dear. It always will be."

The temptation was almost more than she could resist, but somehow she forced out the words. "Jess, I know I'm welcome, and I love you all for it, but I'm still leaving. Nothing will change my mind. I'll stop by tomorrow morning to kiss everyone goodbye."

Later that night she sat before the white wicker desk in her room and took up pen and paper. Surely this was the hardest thing she had ever done in her entire life. She felt like a coward leaving Dan a note, but no way could she tell him goodbye face to face. She was afraid he would try to dissuade her, afraid she'd give in. It would be safer to leave him a note and be on her way before he came down in the morning. With an aching heart, she wrote in a firm, decisive hand that she had decided it would be best for both of them to go their separate ways, that it wasn't fair to him for her to stay on at Kendall's Eden, taking up his time and his life. She was leaving him free to find a wife who could make him happy.

She fought back hot tears that brimmed on her eyelids.

Never again would she know the warm, wonderful feeling of Dan's arms about her. Never again would she know the thrill and excitement of his kiss. Never again would she see him. Life without him would seem empty, meaningless. A searing pain flooded through her, consuming her with sadness. But she mustn't look back. She must put her old life, old memories behind her and move forward. She would drive to Palm Air headquarters in Tampa and ask to be put back on the schedule. She knew she would be on six months' probation. If she blew it, well, she thought grimly, unless she tried, she'd never know if she could fly.

Tears trickled down her cheeks as she finished her note to Dan. She hoped with all her heart that he would find someone to make him happy. With an impatient hand, she swiped at the unwelcome tears. Firmly, she told herself they were only tears of disappointment that living at Kendall's Eden had failed to solve her problems. Ready or not, it was time to be on her own.

Ashly awoke the next morning feeling hot, sticky, and filled with anxiety. The sheet twisted about her waist and hips, clung damply to her body. The September sun high in the sky beat down with merciless heat. Thinking of what she had to do, she felt weighed down, as though she carried the world on her back. She lay in bed watching small clouds scurry across the sky. Puffs of wind rattled the tall Australian pine whose branches beat a nervous tattoo on the roof overhead. Now she wished she'd closed the glass door and turned on the air conditioning last night before going to bed. She lay there in the quiet of the morning staring at the hard, bright sky, and frowned fiercely to stave off tears that burned behind her eyelids.

Sighing deeply, she dragged herself from her bed, slipped into a flowered kimono, and stepped out onto the deck. The air felt unusually hot and oppressive, matching her mood. Even the birds were silent. Glancing overhead, she saw that the sun was now hidden in a haze, a sheet of blinding white light. The strange feeling crept over her that the entire world was standing still and silent, watching, waiting for her to move. She could put it off no longer. Dan would soon be awake and she wanted to be well out of here before he showed up.

With grim resolve she stepped back inside, showered then dressed in a green-and-blue-striped polo shirt and khaki skirt. She took special care with her make-up and hair, donned a pair of gold shell earrings, dabbed perfume behind each ear. She had packed her suitcase last night. Now, as ready as she'd ever be, she hurried down to the kitchen. She stopped short in the doorway. Her breath caught in her throat.

Dan, wearing a bright red t-shirt and cut-offs, sat at the kitchen table, one eye on the grapefruit he was devouring, the other on a portable TV on the counter. He greeted her with an abstracted nod.

Her nerve almost deserted her. How could she leave him a goodbye note? How could she avoid the confrontation she dreaded? Disconcerted, she crossed to the coffee-maker. Trying to keep her voice steady, she asked, "Ready for coffee?" At his nod, she filled two mugs and sat down across from him at the table. His attention was riveted on the news.

Quietly, she said, "Dan, I want to speak with you."

"Speak," he said, not looking at her.

"I mean, seriously."

"I'm listening."

"You're listening to the news."

Looking unusually solemn, he turned to face her. "They're talking about a tropical storm off the Windward Islands. It's driving northward toward Key West, and gale warnings are up from Tampa Bay, south." He turned back to the TV.

She ran her tongue over dry lips. Firmly she said, "Dan, I've decided it's time for me to go."

Still he did not look at her. "Go where?"

"Away—to Tampa."

His eyes on the TV screen, he asked, "What do you want to go to Tampa for?"

"I'm going for—" the word burst from her lips, "—forever."

He turned to face her, his blond, bristly brows arcing in dismay. "I thought you wanted to talk seriously."

"I am serious." Suddenly the words tumbled out like waves breaking on shore. "It isn't fair for me to take up your time, your life. I'm leaving so you'll be free to find a woman who can make you happy and content."

He looked astonished. "I am happy and content."

Softly she said, "Dan, I'm leaving today. Now."

He stared at her, thunderstruck. His eyes bored into hers with piercing intensity.

Sounding slightly hysterical, she plunged on. "I want to go now!" Her voice broke. Close to panic, she thought, *I must go now, before I lose my nerve.*

Dan jumped to his feet and leaned across the table. Gripping her shoulders, he jerked his head toward the TV. "They've added a hurricane warning to the gale and storm warning advisories." His tone turned pleading. "Ashly, you can't go now, or ever!"

Numbly she looked at a radar map on the TV screen that showed the path of the storm, heard the announcer urge residents to evacuate the island as quickly as possible.

"I'm leaving. Now."

He stared at her, his face mirroring shock and disbelief. "You can't mean that, Ashly. I thought that here at Kendall's Eden you'd found peace and contentment and love. I thought I could help you shake your nightmares, your panic attacks, and that you were the answer to my loneliness, that all you needed was time." His eyes turned bleak and he threw up his hands in a helpless gesture. "I see now that rehabilitating animals is a helluva lot different from mending people's lives. There's no way I can dispel memories, fight ghosts . . ." He took a deep breath, as if struggling to regain his composure.

When she said nothing, he went on, his voice harsh,

stinging, like the wind whipping through the pines. "I won't hold you captive. Go!"

She stood stunned, staring at him. Into the charged silence droned the voice of the weather forecaster. "The hurricane warning has been extended along the Gulf Coast from Saint Marks, Florida, to Biloxi, Mississippi. Hurricane Hallie has now centered thirty-five miles off the Florida Keys. Gulf Coast residents are advised—"

In tight, tense tones, Dan said, "We can count on only six to twelve hours lead time at most, so you'd better hurry. I'll drive you to the mainland, but let's make it fast. I have to stop at the Center to square things away, and then I have to batten down here."

Ashly drew herself up, proud and defiant. "You don't have to drive me anywhere. I told Jessamine I'd stop to say goodbye. If you let me take the MG, I'm sure Ted will be glad to drive it back. That will save you time—" She paused, awaiting his approval, but he was listening to the TV announcer reeling off safety precautions to be taken by residents. "I'll get my luggage." Ashly turned and hurried from the kitchen.

She refused to worry about Hurricane Hallie. Jessamine had told her about these hurricane warnings, how years ago everyone had been so frightened when David and Frederic had threatened Sanibel. The entire island battened down like crazy against "the big breeze," and all they suffered was a little wind and rain. "A fake showdown," Jessamine had said, "The advisories tend to overwarn. How many times can they cry wolf?" She gave a wry smile. "But it's like buying car insurance. Better to batten down than spend a bundle rebuilding."

No doubt battening down was better than being caught unprepared, thought Ashly dismally, but she wasn't going to flip because there *might* be a "big breeze."

She looked up to see Dan standing in the doorway watching her with worried eyes and a grim, twisted smile. "Are you ready?"

Wordlessly, she nodded.

He stood jingling the change in his pocket, glancing at his watch every few seconds.

Ashly bit her lip to keep from crying out at the stabbing pain inside her. He's all but pushing me out the door, she thought miserably. How relieved he must be that I'm finally leaving. She zipped the top of her carry-on. As he picked it up and strode out, her fingers curled tightly around the junonia shell deep in her skirt pocket.

In frigid silence they rode the elevator down to the garage. When Dan had stashed her luggage in the trunk of the MG and she had settled into the bucket seat, he handed her the keys.

"Drive directly to Jessamine's. I called to tell them you're on your way, but somebody's yakking on the line. If they're evacuating to the mainland, you take the MG and go. And don't worry about returning it."

He leaned down and kissed her cheek and a look of pain flashed into his eyes, then disappeared so quickly that she wasn't sure she'd seen it. He raised one hand in mock salute and punched the wall button that raised the door. As she backed into the turnaround, he lowered it, and Ashly felt he had shut a final door. She had to muster every ounce of her willpower not to gun the motor and race down the long, narrow lane.

At the San-Cap Road she came to a dead stop, gaping at the scene before her. Cars, trucks, jeeps, loaded with people and pets, their belongings poking out windows or tied on rooftops. Others pulling trailers piled high with lamps, bikes, and furniture crawled bumper to bumper down the road. She started as sirens blared to alert residents to the evacuation.

These poor people, she thought, shaking her head. Panicking because of a hurricane that will probably never strike. She tapped her fingers impatiently on the steering wheel, waiting for a break in the line of cars. She too, was desperate to leave the island, for a far different reason. Just then, an elderly gentleman with frightened blue eyes motioned her forward. She guided the MG into the caravan of cars that crept down the road. It was unbelievable how many islanders were taking the warning to heart. Jessamine probably wouldn't, she thought, reassured. Jessamine knew how capricious the weather could be.

Still, the wind had picked up. The swaying Australian pines that lined the road bowed deeply, their branches bending in an arc overhead. Ashly flicked on the car radio. Announcers blared instruction for evacuation, for safety precautions to be taken by those determined to stay, followed by the location of shelters throughout the county.

At Tarpon Bay Road, she swung right, past the shopping center where men were nailing boards over glass store fronts. Her eyes widened in astonishment. The parking lot was jammed, and people were hurrying in and out of Bailey's. Stocking up on food, thought Ashly abstractedly. Not a bad idea. Maybe Jess could use extra food. She pulled into the parking lot. Inside, long lines of shoppers were loading food into carts as if there were no tomorrow. The store was fast selling out. More than an hour later, Ashly emerged from Bailey's carrying three full bags.

A second caravan of cars laden down with people and possessions crept up Tarpon Bay Road to join others streaming down Periwinkle Way toward the causeway. Thank heaven she was going against traffic, down Tarpon Bay to Jess's cottage. By the time she turned down Gulf Drive, the back of her neck ached with tension. It had taken all her courage to break with Dan. Their disastrous confrontation had left her feeling totally defeated. Worse, this unlikely hurricane threatened to keep her from following through on her resolve to make a new start. She tightened her grip on the wheel. No way would she let a storm deter her.

She pulled into Jessamine's driveway, cut the motor and sat staring at the house, dumbfounded. Every window was crisscrossed with wide bands of tape. The birdbath, lawn chairs, and pots of geraniums were gone from the yard. Even Jessamine, who refused to believe in hurricanes, had taken the warning to heart and battened down.

The door of the house next door flew open and a plump, bald-headed, worried-looking man ran toward her. "If you're looking for Jess and Ted, they've gone." He leaned on the door of the MG. "You must be her sister. She told me to be on the lookout for you. Said to tell you she would've stayed. She doesn't think the storm will amount to a hill of beans. But Ted wouldn't take any chances—says his baby Rosie isn't going to do battle with any hurricane." The man shook his head. "You never know. The weather bureau says to leave. The wife and I are heading out, soon as she empties the fridge."

Ashly nodded, disappointment surging through her.

"You leaving?"

Ashly forced a smile. "I was going to go with whatever Jess and Ted decided, but now—"

The man's worried expression deepened. "Well, if the wife doesn't load too much stuff in the car—" He threw up his hands. "Oh, hell. We'll squeeze you in. People are more important than anything we've got. You come on with us. A warning is a warning. They don't give 'em for no reason. Better safe than sorry. Shouldn't anyone stay on this island that doesn't have to."

Alarm surged through her. Dan was staying. He had to stay, or thought he did. His words, "I have to batten down here," pounded in her head. Smiling, Ashly shook her head. "Thanks, but I have to be on my way."

As she guided the MG down Gulf Road again, angry gusts of wind battered the little car hugging the road. She began to feel uneasy. Anxiety tingled through her. When she would have turned up Tarpon Bay still clogged with evacuees, she forged straight ahead. Maybe traffic would have thinned at the next intersection that lead to the San-Cap Road. She sped past condos and motels. All appeared deserted. Apparently they had been evacuated, for only a few heavily laden cars were charging toward town. When she drew to a stop at San-Cap Road, her heart sank. It was even more congested than before, with every sort of vehicle

DREAM OF LOVE 119

imaginable creeping bumper to bumper in a double column toward the causeway—lifeline to the mainland.

Nervously Ashly glanced at her watch. What with shopping for food and the snail-paced traffic, it had taken more than an hour to drive to Jessamine's. Dan had probably gone to the Center and returned home by now. He surely knew how to take care of himself, but still she was worried.

As she waited to break into the line of cars, the winds rose, gusting menacingly. Billowing black clouds scurried overhead, darkening the sky, blotting the sun from sight. People on last-minute errands scuttled along the streets, bent double against the wind.

A tanned blond woman slowed her car, motioning to Ashly to pull in ahead of her. Ashly floored the gas pedal and shot forward. Without knowing she was going to, instead of falling into line, she spun the wheel sharp left into the far lane. Calmly, deliberately, she drove westward toward Kendall's Eden.

Ten minutes later she braked in the turnaround and pressed the garage door opener. As the door rose slowly upward, her attention was caught by a flicker of motion in the rearview mirror. The next instant she glimpsed a flash of red and a surge of joy swept through her. Dan, in his red t-shirt, a birdcage clutched to his chest, his lean, tough body bent into the wind, was making his way through the swaying trees. Ashly jumped from the car and ran to meet him.

His mouth fell open in dismay. "What in hell are you doing here?"

"I—I," she started to say, "I came back to persuade you to leave," but upset by his words, she stammered, "Jess—Jessamine and Ted have gone. They must have left just before I got there."

Dan shook his head, an incredulous expression in his dark blue eyes. "Then why didn't you follow the evacuation route, the blue-and-white signs, off the island? Good grief, you were within spitting distance of the causeway!"

Tremulously, she said, "I came back to help you batten

down, to pack up the birds and animals." Her voice rose, urgent, pleading. "We have to hurry, have to leave the island. Jess's neighbor said *everyone* should leave. It's crazy to stay, when—"

Roughly, Dan interrupted. "You're crazy to have driven back here, risking your own neck." The worry in his eyes as he looked at her belied his harsh words. "I can't leave. Even if I could carry the menagerie to the mainland, what would I do with them?"

"The zoo—"

"The zoo will have enough casualties without my bringing in more animals." His voice hardened in tones of command. "So climb back in that car and get the hell out of here, while the getting's good!"

He swung around her, stepped inside the elevator and the doors slid closed, shutting him from sight.

Devastated, Ashly whipped open the door of the MG, flung herself into the seat and turned the key in the ignition. Dan's heated warning, "Get the hell out of here while the getting's good!" echoed and re-echoed in her mind. She blinked back tears. Did he want her to leave before the storm hit; or before he held her captive once again?

Her lips set in a stubborn line. All her life she had listened to other people: to Jessamine, Ted, and Werner, and had let them influence her. Now Dan told her what to do. She reached toward the ignition and withdrew the key.

Chapter 12

Smiling a small, secret smile, Ashly punched the button to open the garage door, then pulled in beside the Rolls. She ran outside, lowered the garage door, and dashed through wind-tossed trees to the rustic log cabin. First she would help Dan carry his charges to safety.

Inside the cabin, she raced from room to room in dismay. Except for three infant raccoons in a wicker basket, all the birds and animals were gone. Deciding that Dan had probably stashed them in the game room on the ground floor, she draped a towel over the basket, picked it up and hurried out, shutting the cabin door firmly after her.

Heavy, moist air pressed around her, clinging like an invisible sheath. Tree branches swayed low, their leaves turned inside out. Sea oats whipped her legs as she dashed back to the house.

Quickly she scanned the game room and sauna and saw no sign of Dan's animals. She rode the elevator upstairs and as the doors slid open, drew back with a start. The setter and the lab bounded into the foyer to greet her, tails beating the air. Strange sounds interspersed with loud quacks drew her toward the kitchen. At the threshold she stopped short, gaping in surprise.

The owl's box stood in one corner beside a chicken-wire pen. Inside, stood a small blue heron beside a nest which held two blue eggs. A scrawny brown rabbit with a ragged ear hopped curiously around the top of the island counter. All Dan's patients were here: the white egret strutted around a big wire cage; the black snake snoozed in his gallon pickle jar; the tiger-striped tabby was curled up on her cushion in a corner. Ashly's astonished gaze swept past sacks of feed, cans of dog and cat food, a bale of straw, a pile of old blankets, and a wooden crate that held a first aid box and medical supplies from the cabin.

It was the blue-winged teal making such a fuss, emitting raucous quacks from her wide-open bill. Ashly's gaze riveted on Dan and her breath caught in her throat. He stood at the counter bent over the teal, murmuring soothing sounds as he tried to hold it still. Last week the vet had set the duck's broken wing. Now the binding had come loose and the other chalky blue wing flapped frantically.

She set the basket of baby raccoons on the tiled floor and between squawks, said in crisp, light tones, "I take it this is the infirmary."

Dan wheeled to face her, his eyes filled with mingled astonishment and concern. In three quick strides, he crossed the room, placed his hands on her shoulders, and looked worriedly into her eyes. "Ashly, I thought you'd gone. What on earth are you doing here?"

"I'm staying. I'm your assistant, remember?"

A tender expression came over his face. As if regretting the hurtful words he'd spoken earlier, he said softly, "You're kind, courageous, and crazy, my love, but you have to go. If anything happened to you, I'd never forgive myself." The blue teal quacked loudly.

As if Dan hadn't spoken, Ashly smiled and above the duck's strident honks, shouted, "You forgot the raccoons."

Dan turned back to the teal. It stared at them with terrified, shining black eyes as his fingers closed firmly

DREAM OF LOVE

around its squawking bill. In the sudden silence Dan shouted, "I was going back for the raccoons when I finished here." His voice turned gruff. "Please, Ashly, listen to me. Go, before you get caught in the deluge."

She shook her head. "I hear what you're saying, but I'm not going."

Dan's mouth dropped open as he stood gaping at her in disbelief.

In calm, confident tones, she said, "I'm staying—to help you batten down. Let's have at it."

Forgetting to hold the blue teal's bill, he flung out his hands in protest. "Absolutely not, Ashly. It's too risky."

The duck squawked wildly, interrupting him.

"I can't let you stay!" Dan shouted. The duck nipped his forefinger. Again his hand closed around the lethal bill.

Ashly's lips curved in an implacable smile. "You can't leave the island with me, so I'll ride out the storm with you."

Dan stared at her for a long moment, then let out a helpless sigh. "You *know* I can't leave. When I finish here, I'll be needed to help rescue stranded animals—" His expression hardened, "—and other stubborn fools who don't go when they're told." More gently he said, "You're really mule-headed, you know."

Ashly grinned. "And you're not?" Leaning against the cabinet, she folded her arms across her chest in an attitude of patient waiting.

Dan scowled down at the terrified teal. Finally he muttered, "Will you hold her while I fix this splint?"

Ashly held the duck while Dan secured the splint. She recalled how gentle, how tender his hands could be, how their touch set her every nerve-ending on fire. Her throbbing heart seemed to keep pace with the bird's wildly beating pulse.

When they finished treating the duck, Ashly held the rabbit and Dan swabbed its torn ear. Now she became aware that the animals were moving restlessly about, acting nervous and upset as if they sensed danger from the approaching storm. She helped Dan settle them down, stroking, talking, calming them as best she could.

The day outside grew leaden, gulf and sky seeming to merge in a vast, steel-gray cauldron. The wind blew foamy whitecaps from the crests of the waves and whipped through the trees, buffeting the house. Dan glanced out the window at the threatening sky. "Damn! I didn't have time to bring in the outdoor stuff. I'll tend to it. You stay here."

Ashly nodded, and followed him from the house.

Dan raced about the grounds gathering up garden tools and trash cans, and carried redwood boxes of scarlet geraniums and potted plants inside to the foyer. Ashly dashed to the pool deck and collected the flowered cushions from the furniture. Together they hauled chairs, tables, chaise, and umbrella to the concrete block storage room. Through the stilts that supported the house, the wind soughed with an eerie, whining sound that made Ashly's scalp prickle. With a growing sense of urgency, they moved faster, hurrying to outrun the storm. As they carried in the last yellow metal chair, the first spattering of rain fell.

Ashly nodded toward the garage. "While we're down here, we'd better bring in my luggage and the food I brought along."

Smiling, Dan shook his head in wonder. "You think of everything, my love. In fact, you are the woman I'd most like to be stranded on a desert island with."

Ashly grinned back at him. "You only love me for my groceries from Bailey's." Carrying two plastic gallon jugs of bottled water, she stepped inside the elevator.

In the kitchen they put the food away, pausing now and then to catch the latest weather advisories on TV. Absently Ashly listened to the calm, controlled voice of the forecaster. ". . . an intense hurricane with fiercely spiraling winds estimated as high as one hundred miles per hour skirting the western tip of Cuba . . . warnings extended farther west to New Orleans."

On the screen flashed pictures taken by hurricane hunter planes flying above a towering column of rain clouds that swirled around the center of Hurricane Hallie. Others showed a whirling sphere with flying tails that looked like something out of a science fiction movie. Ashly shivered and turned her head away.

"No way to predict the path of Hurricane Hallie," said the announcer in smooth, matter-of-fact tones, as if he were reporting a ball game and was hesitant to predict the outcome. "Hallie's speed, too, may vary. She may stand motionless for awhile, spinning like a monstrous top, or she may reach forward speeds of forty miles per hour. Hurricanes sometimes turn at right angles to their former path, or they can zigzag in an erratic—"

Ashly stopped listening. She felt no premonition of danger. It seemed as if they were watching a typical TV program, a pregame show before the Super Bowl, or an old movie, not an actual event to be taken seriously. She knew that the Hurricane Center had to warn residents along the entire coastal area; that they were all threatened, since no one could tell where a hurricane would strike. Privately, she thought Hallie could well be another of Jessamine's "fake showdowns." And when Dan suggested they start preparing for the "big blow," Ashly, to keep Dan happy, helped him batten down.

They spent the morning and much of the afternoon crisscrossing acres of windows with huge rolls of tape—protection against shards of flying glass if the windows were blown out. They nailed plywood to windows they could reach, ran water in the bathtubs, then gathered up candles and matches. From the storage room, Dan brought a giant thermos, an old green camp stove, a lantern and a red can of kerosene. He rummaged through the kitchen drawers and found extra batteries for a long chromium flashlight he kept on hand for emergencies.

Shortly after three, they moved into the living room where Dan switched on the lamps and TV and sank down on the couch. Ashly, standing before the glass doors looking out over the Gulf, began to feel uneasy. "The sky *is* growing darker, and the waves are breaking higher on the beach."

In strong confident tones, Dan said, "Not to worry. We're ready for whatever Hallie hands out."

Ashly shivered and wrapped her arms about her as the wind gusted fiercely, howling about the house, screaming through the trees. Beside the sundeck, swaying cabbage palms, their fronds like skirts blowing over their heads, made an eerie tapping on the roof, as if demanding to come inside. Mesmerized, Ashly gazed at the angry waves lashing the beach, then glanced anxiously over her shoulder at Dan. "It must be later than I thought. The water is already up to the high tide mark."

Dan crossed to stand beside her, scowling at the tempestuous scene before them. "High tide isn't till after four. The winds are pushing the water up on shore. And those black, mountainous clouds make it seem like night coming on." He curved an arm about her shoulders and gave her a reassuring hug.

"We're completely safe here. The house stands on a rise, and we're a good twenty-five feet above sea level."

As they stood in silent awe watching the violent winds, Dan's brow furrowed in an anxious frown. "What really concerns me is Jessamine's house and the others strung out along Gulf Road. They could wash away like toy blocks."

Ashly nodded. "I'm worried about them too, but I'm so grateful that Ted took Jessamine and Rosie away—"

She broke off, sure Dan would say she should have gone as well. Instead, he said, "It's almost four. The Hurricane Center in Miami should issue an update advisory. Let's see what Hallie's up to."

Together they sank down on the soft velvet beige couch. He draped an arm about her shoulders in a comforting way that made her want to snuggle closer and rest her head on his chest. She forced herself to listen to the forecast.

In grave tones the announcer said, "The storm has crept northward and at eleven P.M. is expected to be south of the Everglades, moving close to the coastline tomorrow. The winds should reach hurricane force by morning, striking Naples by mid-afternoon. Meteorologists predict that the center of the fierce storm will be about eighty miles southwest of Fort Myers."

Ashly began to feel edgy and apprehensive. Her anxiety mounted as they watched on-the-scene reports showing cars, pick-ups and trailers rolling off the causeway into boarded-up Fort Myers. A tense-faced reporter said authorities hoped these were the last of the evacuees, for in many places the road was covered with water, impassable now, with tides three to six feet above normal. A number of Australian pines were struck down, uprooted, blocking the escape route, trapping carloads of residents behind the fallen trees. Others had fled to shelters. Viewers were advised to keep tuned for further bulletins. As the man signed off, Ashly became suddenly aware that the wind was growing louder, roaring about the house like a freight train barreling down a track. Dan got to his feet, his expression grim.

"I'm going to open the windows on the lee side of the house to keep the pressure down inside. You keep an ear on the news and let me know if Hallie changes direction."

After Dan had gone, Ashly, drawn to the double glass doors, stood looking out, appalled at the havoc wrought by the wind and water. In the glare of white flashes of lightning she saw tree limbs snapped like matchsticks, thick branches downed like twigs. A green beach chair bearing the monogram of a motel miles down the beach whirled past. Monstrous waves driven by a vicious wind crashed on the shore and washed up on land as if pursuing an enemy.

Glancing downward, Ashly let out a horrified gasp. The raging waters had climbed the rise, drowned the sea oats, crept up the grassy lawn and submerged the pool. The entire terrace was a dark, windswept lake tossing to and fro. A tremor shook her. Dampness penetrated every corner of the room and she felt chilled clear through. She wrapped her arms about her, as if to ward off the fear and dread rising inside her.

She had no idea how long she had been standing there, watching the ravaging winds and water in what seemed the half-light of the underworld, when the heavy woven draperies began to close in on her. Startled, she spun around. Dan, tugging at the cord, grinned at her.

"Let's shut out the night."

"Night! How can you tell!"

Dan tapped his watch. "It's feeding time on the ark." He grasped her arm and turned her from the window. She cast an apprehensive glance over her shoulder and saw the draperies swaying, stirred by the wind that seeped through the glass. Dan managed a smile that didn't mask the concern in his eyes.

"Come along, friend. Talk to the animals."

Falling in with his determinedly cheerful mood, she joked, "Doctor Dolittle, I presume." Then quickly added, "Nothing personal, of course."

With a lopsided grin, he said, "I hope I don't *look* like the ancient and venerable Doctor Doolittle."

Ashly's eyes sparkled with amusement. "There's nothing wrong with being ancient and venerable."

Dan cocked an eyebrow at her. "Even if you're thirty-two?"

"Thirty-two! All this time I thought you were crowding fifty."

"For that disrespectful remark," said Dan laughing, "you draw eyedropper duty for the infant raccoons. They like their milk warmed in the microwave."

Dan gave the barn owl a glob of hamburger, poured grain for the birds, and fed the dogs and his other wildlife refugees. When he had finished, he stood quietly watching Ashly feed the raccoons. Sensing his gaze on her, she turned to face him and saw a tender expression flash across his face and quickly disappear.

Cheerfully he asked, "And what gourmet dish do you want the creative cook to prepare for your dinner?"

An impish smile curved her lips. Eyeing the blue-winged teal, she said, "I think—duck l'orange."

Dan grinned. "I'd be happy to oblige, if we had an orange. Instead, we'll have fresh red snapper my fisherman friend gave me. Thinks I'm starving, and he drops by the Center daily to leave me his catch." Dan opened the door and reached inside the lighted fridge. His hand halted mid-air as the light went out and the room was plunged into darkness.

Chapter 13

Through the darkness came a low, mournful call. A chill ran up Ashly's spine and her hands tightened protectively around the baby raccoon in her lap.

"Damn!" Dan muttered. "Even the owl is nervous."

She heard him rummaging over the countertop. "Where the devil are those candles?"

Ashly fumbled around the floor for the wicker basket and set the raccoon inside. She rose to her feet and, hands outstretched before her, started across the kitchen.

"Help is on the way." Blindly she groped toward the counter, touched a can opener, toaster, canisters, the first aid box. As her hands closed around the flashlight, she sensed Dan's warm, solid figure close to hers. She turned slightly. Flesh and bone collided. She let out a gasp. Dan's strong arms closed around her as if to keep her from falling. Taken by surprise, she burst out, "Dan, is that you?"

He gave a low chuckle. "Right. Who's this?"

His breath, warm on her cheek, his lips close to hers, made her tingle all over. Unsteadily, she murmured, "It isn't the Avon Lady."

"What a disappointment!"

Despite his attempt at lightness, anxiety rose like gorge in her throat. The darkness, the unrelenting roar of the wind, the tumult of water, unnerved her. Her palms grew damp, her heart pounded. Old, remembered fear quickened, surged through her. Sternly she told herself, "It's not the same as floundering in an icy river!" Still, memory mocked her and the storm outside seemed to rage inside her. A shiver shook her. She bit her lip hard, forcing down panic. Dan's arms tightened around her, his chin pressed against her hair. His voice, warm and reassuring, cut through the darkness.

"Don't worry, darling, we're in great shape. This house was built to withstand hurricanes, cyclones, tornadoes, all acts of God and the devil. We're well above high water. All that pounding is only the wind whipping through the stilts."

Mindlessly Ashly clung to him, molding her body to his. She wished he would never let her go, for here in his arms was the only place in the world she felt truly safe. Her heart was beating so hard she was sure he must feel it thudding against his chest.

He placed his hands on her shoulders as if to put her from him. She wanted to cry out, "Dan, please, I know everything is over between us, but just hold me." She kept silent, clinging to him with desperation born of love and fear. He clasped her shoulders firmly, and drawing back from her, kissed her brow, each eyelid, the tip of her nose.

She raised her head, and her mouth, eager, seeking, found his in a plea to prolong their embrace, to reassure her. She felt his sharp intake of breath and his lips touched hers in tentative response. Gently he ran a hand down her back and with his free hand, smoothed a tendril of hair from her temple. He traced the curve of her cheek, neck, and throat, around the fullness of her breast. With his thumb and forefinger he stroked, teased the flesh to life, igniting fires that smoldered deep in her soul.

"Dan, Dan," she murmured, thrilling to his caress. She

knew she should tell him to stop now, before she was swept up in an intimacy she was helpless to resist. Weakly, she whispered a feeble protest against lips so warm and demanding on her own.

His kiss deepened, his tongue exploring, tasting the sweetness of her mouth. His hand on her back strayed downward, pressed her warm, supple body tightly against his, so that she was vividly aware that his throbbing, surging desire matched her own, that any moment their passions would override all reason.

Summoning every ounce of willpower she possessed, Ashly pulled away from him and switched on the flashlight. A circle of pale white light flooded the floor at their feet. Ashly started, stifling a cry of alarm. Glowing at her through the darkness were eyes—bright, shining yellow eyes, frightened, solemn, menacing eyes, and eyes burning red in the darkness.

She played the light around the room over the bird cages, the owl's box and the duck pen, to the dogs sprawled on their blankets. In a desperate attempt to relieve the tension between them, she said in dry, hoarse tones, "Do you have the feeling we're being watched?"

Dan's low laughter filled the room. Ashly flashed the light upward, catching him in its beam. Her heart skipped a beat. His face was flushed, his eyes burning with an emotion she couldn't name. Disappointment, frustration, anger?

Gently, he nudged her chin and took the flashlight from her hand. "We'd better have some light." Although he spoke in a bantering tone, the huskiness in his voice told her that he had been swept by emotions that matched her own—and what it cost him to suppress them.

The flashlight's beam skimmed along the counter to a collection of candles in brass, silver, and glass holders. Dan handed Ashly a folder of matches, took up another and began to light the candles. Her hand shook so, she could scarcely hold flame to wick. She glanced at Dan, wondering if he had noticed. He was staring hard at a match flame, his hand no steadier than her own.

Despite the fury raging outside, the glow from the forest of lighted tapers lent a warmth and cheerfulness to the kitchen. Within minutes Dan was sautéing red snapper fillets and stirring up a pan of frozen string beans on the camp stove. Ashly tossed together a green salad with lettuce, hearts of palm, mushrooms, and a tangy blue cheese dressing, then sliced a loaf of crusty French bread. She saw Dan watching her as she spread each slice with garlic butter. She smiled up at him.

"Hot garlic bread all right with you?"

He nodded toward the oven. "No juice. The oven went out with the lights."

Ashly slid the beans from the camp stove burner, speared a slice of bread on a long-handled fork and began toasting it over the low, blue flame. Smiling, she said, "There's more than one way to skin a cat."

Dan scowled in mock disapproval. "Please! Don't speak of skinning cats to a conservationist."

Amusement sparkled in Ashly's light blue eyes. "Sorry, I forgot you're an animal lover."

"Definitely. They're a helluva lot more loyal and dependable than people."

With a vehemence that surprised her, she said, "You bet!" The next instant she thought, *I'm overreacting! This miserable weather is giving me the jitters.* In the sudden silence, the roar of the winds, battering the house seemed to fill her ears and a paralyzing fear squeezed her heart.

"Watch it!" Dan shouted. He grabbed the fork from her hand and blew out the flames blackening the bread. "I'll do the bread. You set the table."

Ashly looked about her at the birdcages on the table, the owl's box and pens on the floor, the bright-eyed rabbit crouched on a chair. A host of eyes watched their every move.

Lightly, she said, "Do you mind dining in private, in the living room?"

Dan grinned. "Whatever your heart desires."

She placed lighted candles, red linen place mats, silverware, and two china plates on a bamboo tray and carried it into the living room. She set two places side by side on the glass table before the velvet couch. Unaccountably, in the face of threatened disaster, she felt a need to serve their meal beautifully, to keep up the pretense of a festive dinner, as if by doing so, she could stave off catastrophe. An ironic smile curved her lips. How fitting, she thought, that a hurricane should mark the end of their idyll.

Dan strode into the room carrying a tray of food and a bottle of chablis, sank down on the couch beside her, and filled two glasses with the clear sparkling wine. Smiling deeply into her eyes, he raised his glass. "To your happiness."

Ashly's gaze locked with his. Forcing a smile, she murmured, "To *your* happiness!" She touched the rim of her glass to his, and to her annoyance, unbidden tears shimmered in her eyes. Quickly she blinked them back, staring hard at the food on her plate. With a determinedly cheerful air, she devoured light, flaky snapper garnished with lemon and parsley, crisp, crunchy beans almondine and juicy thin-sliced garden tomatoes.

"My compliments to the chef," said Ashly admiringly. "I'm impressed."

Dan's eyes twinkled. "Your salad was terrific and the French bread wasn't half bad. Just the right texture, beautifully sliced—"

Ashly laughed. "—And toasted to perfection!"

Strangely, she felt totally relaxed. She supposed it was because having at last made the decision to leave him, she no longer anticipated their future together. Dan, too, appeared much more at ease. No doubt he was relieved that the strain of living under the same roof would soon end, she thought dispiritedly. Free from tension, they could enjoy each other's company.

They lingered over cups of fragrant coffee that Ashly made on the camp stove and talked of various projects at the Center. Resolutely they ignored the sounds of the raging winds, the pounding surf, until their attention was distracted by the ship's clock chiming ten.

Sighing, Dan said, "We'd better see where Hallie's hanging out." He rose and flicked on the TV. Nothing happened. Ashly shook her head. Dan hurried from the room and returned with a transistor radio. He flicked the dial. "I'm trying to find WRCC at Cape Coral. They broadcast official emergency information for Sanibel."

Ashly sighed inwardly. For a short while they had shut out the night, the treacherous winds and waters, the rain slashing against the windows, the havoc raging outside. Now, good news or bad, the radio would intrude, would destroy this pleasant interlude that she hated to see end.

Silent, apprehensive, they listened to the weather report. Hurricane Hallie, which had been spinning around the mouth of the Gulf, was headed northwest and would probably smash inland somewhere between Mississippi and Louisiana. Forecasters were now certain that it would avoid the Florida coast. The southern section of Florida, though still under hurricane warnings, was in danger mostly from tornadoes spinning off the sides of the swirling masses of clouds. Locally, gale force winds were still buffeting Sanibel-Captiva Island.

Dan leaned back against the couch and gave a long, relieved sigh. "Guess we don't have to worry that Hallie will strike while we're asleep. We'd better turn in. It's been a long day." Smiling, he took Ashly's hand in his and pulled her to her feet. "I'll light your way to your room." He picked up the flashlight and nodded toward two flaming candles in brass holders. "Better take those along," his smile broadened, "unless you can see in the dark. There are no candles in your room."

Candles. So romantic, she thought wistfully, and instantly reminded herself that their romance was over and done. As she started toward the elevator, Dan grasped her elbow firmly. He led her toward the white, curved wrought-iron stairway.

The shining brass candlesticks trembled in her hands. Dan slid his flashlight into his back pocket, took one of the candlesticks, and curved his free arm about her waist, drawing her close against his side. Ashly held her breath, steeling herself against the dizzying sensation of the warmth of his body next to her own.

Holding their candles high, they mounted the stairs in silence. Ashly, watching their shadows dancing on the ivory walls in the flickering candlelight, reminded herself that this was the last night they would sleep under the same roof. At the thought that their days together were almost at an end an overwhelming sadness surged through her. The pleasant hours they had just passed proved how happy they could be. Was she making another tragic mistake by leaving him? She had been afraid of a new love, afraid to trust her own judgment. Then, when she was sure she loved Dan Kendall, she loved him too much to saddle him with a wife who couldn't get her act together, or control the terrors that beset her.

She should never have returned to Kendall's Eden. But she wasn't sorry she'd come back. She couldn't leave Dan when he needed her. Tomorrow she would be on her way.

They walked down the wide hallway to her room. Wistfully, without intending to, she spoke her thoughts aloud. "This will be our last night together. I mean," she said hastily, blushing, "the last night we both spend under this roof."

Dan stared at her over the yellow candle flame. Mistaking her meaning, he said, "Don't say that! Don't even think it! Hallie wouldn't dare blow the roof off this house!"

He paused at the doorway of her room and she stepped quickly across the threshold, and turned to face him. Softly, she said, "Goodnight, Dan. Sleep well."

"See you in the morning." Gently, he closed the door and was gone.

Quickly she undressed and slipped into her white shorty gown. Seated before the mirror at the dressing table, she picked up a silver-backed brush and began to stroke her hair. Unaccountably, she felt bereft and desperately lonely. Outside, the shrieking winds and lashing rains mounted in strength and fury. Fear consumed her. Her hands grew clammy and she began to tremble all over. The brush slid from her hand. Firmly, she told herself that at this moment, here and now, she was safe. Each moment by itself was always bearable. Moment by moment, she sat very still, staring into the mirror. Without warning, in its depths, she saw her bedroom door swing open. Dan, clad in a maroon knee-length wrap-around robe, stood framed in the doorway.

"Sounds like all hell is breaking loose out there. Are you all right?"

She jumped up from the bench, ran across the room and flung herself into his arms. He curved one arm around her back and held her tightly against his chest. With his free hand, he patted her back until her trembling subsided. Nuzzling her ear he said, "Thought you might need a friend close by."

She wound her arms about his neck and leaned her forehead against his. "I do. Thank you." she murmured.

He kissed the tip of her nose. "You're welcome."

His lips found hers, lingered in a long, gentle kiss. "May I—?"

"Mmmmm—"

His mouth pressed down on hers, forcing her lips apart. Tentatively, her tongue touched his. His kiss deepened, and as his tongue explored the sweetness of her mouth, her ardor matched his own. She strained against the lean, muscular length of his body, feeling as if she could never be close enough. She heard his sharp intake of breath as he held her ever closer, as if in answer to her need.

He slid his hands down her back, curved one arm about her waist, the other under her knees, and carried her to the bed. He eased down on the side of the bed and, as though reluctant to let her go, cuddled her in his lap. He trailed kisses up her neck, her earlobes, her eyelids, then once again his mouth, warm and demanding, sought her own.

Her lips clinging to his, she ran her fingertips lightly over his cheeks, up his temples, through his slightly damp thick, blond hair. His body had a clean, soapy scent, and she realized he must have come to her fresh from a shower. She wound one arm around his neck and slipped her free hand inside his robe. Lovingly, she teased the springy mat of hair that covered his chest. She slid his robe from his shoulders, down his arms, around his waist. Gently, he stroked her breasts, her hips, her thighs. She thrilled to the touch of his hands traveling over her body. Her heart began to pound and the heat from their bodies enveloped them like a warm cloud.

His kiss became more demanding and her breath quickened. He curved an arm around her back and lowered her head and shoulders to the bed so that she lay across his lap. Slowly, he swept her gown upward, over her breasts, slipped it over her head and cast it aside. Without volition, her back arched and she felt as though every nerve ending were on fire. With one finger Dan traced the curves of her breasts, then cupping their fullness in his hands, he kissed one taut rosy peak, then the other.

Gently, he stroked her knees, her thighs, his fingers trailing up and down the length of her slender body until she ached with desire. When he bent his head and buried his face in the soft golden curls above her thighs, she writhed helplessly in his arms.

He shed his robe, then drew her upward, clasping her to his chest. With one easy motion he rolled to the center of the bed. Bracing his body on his elbows, he stretched out above her. His breath was coming in quick gasps and his lips were swollen with the heat of passion. Ashly grasped his shoulders and pulled him into her. As their bodies fused, she cried out in ecstasy. Never had she known such passion, such joy. For the first time in her life, she felt complete. As the storm raging outside grew in intensity, the fervor of their lovemaking rose to match it.

DREAM OF LOVE

With all the pent-up longing and desire they had denied for so many months, set free, they made love again, and again. When at last their passions were spent, they slept entwined in each other's arms.

Chapter 14

Ashly awoke with a feeling of euphoria, basking in the joy of last night's lovemaking with Dan. She turned to look at him, and felt a stab of disappointment. The space beside her was empty. Dan was gone. "No reason to panic," she told herself firmly. He had made her feel like the most desirable, the most beautiful, the most loved woman in the world. She should feel elated. Still, she felt vaguely disturbed, disoriented. Gradually she became aware of an alien sound, an immense dull roar, as of a conch shell pressed against her ear.

She slid from the bed, ran to the glass doors and flung aside the blue chiffon draperies. She stared outward, straining her eyes till they stung. All she could see was a vast, pewter-gray world. Rain, blown by furious winds, falling heavily, horizontally, like millions of fine needles, screened the world from sight. Quickly she closed the draperies to shut out the storm.

However dismal things looked, Ashly decided, she would put on a good face. Perhaps she could recapture the festive mood of last night. She dressed and went downstairs.

She found Dan in the kitchen, barefoot before the camp

stove frying bacon. As if today were like any other rainy day; as if they had not spent last night lost in the rapture of each other's arms; as if everything were under control; as if there were no danger and no need to keep an ear riveted to the National Weather Service bulletins to keep tabs on Hurricane Hallie. He had even turned down the volume on the transistor radio.

Smiling, Ashly crossed to a chair and stroked the ears of the rabbit nibbling pellets. "Which way to the Ark?"

Dan threw her a cheerful grin. "You're on it. Welcome aboard." In teasing tones he went on, "Your timing is terrific. I've just finished swabbing the deck and spreading fresh straw and papers. All the birds and beasts are fed and watered except for you and me. You can have whatever you want as long as it's eggs: scrambled, fried, boiled—"

Mischief gleamed in her eyes. "Coddled, please."

"Coddled! Whoever heard of a coddled egg?"

"I have! I'll show you!" She took two eggs from the yellow bowl on the counter. While Dan finished frying the bacon and Ashly coddled the eggs, they carried on a friendly banter. But when they were seated on the couch before the coffee table in the living room eating breakfast, a silence fell between them. It seemed that all they had to say to each other had been said, thought Ashly morosely.

It's the weather, she decided. This horrible storm hammering away without letup. Despite their determined efforts to be cheerful, gloom and bone-chilling dampness pervaded the house. Her skin felt clammy all over. Dan opened the draperies to let in the morning light, but the day was so gray that they seemed to be enveloped in a fine, pearly mist. The driving rain and roaring winds made Ashly jittery. She got up and lighted the candles, but their brave, bright glow paled in the melancholy half-light of the storm-swept day.

Dan turned up the transistor and in grim silence they listened to the early-morning weather advisory. Hurricane Hallie, playing tag with weather forecasters in the Gulf, was on the move again. She was gradually increasing her speed from fourteen to forty-two miles per hour, and veering northwest. The band of spiraling clouds extended for one hundred miles with winds up to one-hundred-thirty-five miles per hour. To be on the safe side, warnings were extended to the entire Florida coastline, although they expected Hallie to hurtle inland between Pensacola and Tallahassee.

With cheerful optimism, Dan remarked, "Sounds like it'll bypass us. We'll be hit only with peripheral winds, thank God."

"Wonderful!" Ashly forced a smile. Hallie would soon pass, and with her passing, Ashly would move on, leaving the island and Dan behind. A wave of sadness and regret surged through her. She had been unbelievably foolish and naive to come back here to stand by him when she thought he needed her.

Shortly after noon, the weather bureau reported that the eye of the hurricane was wobbling from side to side, shifting from east to west and back again. First it appeared to be headed for New Orleans. Then the capricious eye drifted east, as if bound for Naples, Florida.

Dan shook his head. "Not good. Years ago, during Hurricane Donna, before the storm actually passed, water was drawn from the back bays around Fort Myers Beach and Sanibel. When the storm hit all the water came back like a tidal wave and this caused more damage than the wind. The island was flooded as far up San Carlos Boulevard as Pine Ridge Road. One big danger was the threat of snakes trying to get into the houses for protection. People were shooting them everywhere. Worse, cinderblock homes built on the gulf front were washed away, leaving a big hole in the sand."

"That's incredible. Thank God Jessamine and Ted and Rosie have gone. If Hallie turns on us, do you think we can hang in here?"

Dan reached over and gave her hand a squeeze. "Have to. The good news is that houses built on stilts like this one fared much better."

DREAM OF LOVE 143

"Best news I've heard all day," said Ashly rolling her eyes heavenward.

After they had done all they could to protect Kendall's Eden and themselves, Dan challenged Ashly to a game of gin. With each hour that passed as they whiled away the afternoon, the storm worsened. It came as no surprise when the announcer on the four o'clock advisory reported that Hurricane Hallie had struck Naples with devastating wrath and was sweeping northward toward the tiny island of Sanibel, directly in her path. Ashly dared not voice the fear that filled her heart, and concentrated on the cards.

Shortly before dusk, Dan shuffled the deck with a flourish and glanced down at the score pad. "You're down two games," he said amiably. "I'll give you one more chance to catch me."

"You're on," she said, with a forced enthusiasm she did not feel. She played abstractedly, staring unseeing at the cards. Carefully she avoided Dan's gaze, afraid he'd read the fear in her eyes. Yet she longed to look at him, to etch every line of his face in her memory forever.

Thirty minutes later, Ashly started at the sound of an immense roar. At the same instant, she felt the house shudder under the impact of the hurricane. They didn't need the forecaster to tell them that Hallie was hovering over Sanibel. With elaborate casualness, Dan rose to his feet.

"Let's pack it in. You owe me three-and-a-quarter." He grinned down at her, but he couldn't hide the worry in his eyes. "I'm going to check out the house—all the rooms, windows, roof, crow's nest. Will you be all right here?"

Ashly nodded. Shortly after Dan left, she got up and peered out the glass doors. The rain had stopped. Miraculously, as if on signal from some omnipotent hand, the winds died. She slid open the doors and stepped out onto the wooden deck. She gazed in wonder at a skim-milk sky brightened by patches of blue.

The eye of the storm, she decided. At the same time she recalled the forecaster's strong warning not to be deceived;

not to think the storm had ended and venture out during the lull, for the second half of the hurricane would strike with fierce intensity. But now the world was as calm as a painted sea. With stricken eyes she gazed at the destruction Hallie had wrought. Trees, wild tangles of broken limbs and branches, debris tossed up on shore: a blue-and-white cabana, twisted and torn; a child's yellow tricycle caught in the limbs of a live oak; a washing machine rested in the crotch of an uprooted pine.

From the corner of her eye she saw a flash of movement off to her left. She whipped around. Something white fluttered from the branches of a fallen oak. A towel? A pillowcase flapping in the wind? But there was no wind.

She ran along the deck to the corner of the house for a closer look. The fluttering white shape became wings, a bird caught in the tangled branches, trying to free itself. Her heart went out to the poor creature. She knew how it felt, exhausted from the buffeting winds; felt its entanglement, its hopelessness, its naked panic. She could easily rescue it, run that short distance and back again before the eye of the hurricane passed over.

She kicked off her sandals, tucked the hem of her skirt into her waistband, then dashed down the outside stairway. At the foot of the stairs she stopped dead, staring in horror at the roiling black river below her. Somewhere in the distance she heard the faint drone of a plane, a hurricane hunter.

Memory quickened. A terrible fear rose inside her. A strangling sensation choked off her breath and a convulsive shiver shook her. A voice in her head shouted, "Think of the bird, only the bird!"

She fixed her gaze resolutely on the white bird fluttering helplessly only yards away. A gull! Certainly not an endangered species, but a suffering creature, within her power to save.

Frantically, she looked around her. Broken, splintered branches poked up from the swirling lake that engulfed the house, and dead birds that had been flung up against the trees were strewn everywhere. Her stomach lurched. Sickened by the sight, she turned her head, then started, her eyes wide with dismay. There, between the pilings under the house, a porpoise was swimming and—the hair on the back of her neck stiffened—she let out a choked cry. Two black snakes slithered through the foam-flecked waters evidently searching for dry land.

With a desperate effort of will she blocked the snakes from her mind and plunged into the foaming water. She clenched her jaw and waded deeper. Gripping fallen limbs and branches, she thrust them out of her way. She forced herself to think only of the hapless bird, riveted her gaze on the flapping wings.

Somewhere behind her she head a shout. Clutching a broken pine branch, she glanced over her shoulder. Dan stood at the railing on the crow's nest waving wildly. His mouth opened and closed, but the roar of the weather plane drowned out his voice.

Ashly waved back, then pointed to the bird. Dan gestured frantically, pointing skyward. Thinking he was calling her attention to the hurricane hunter flying overhead, she nodded, then turned back to the gull. Only a few feet further, and she could free it.

She lunged forward. The water crept higher, stinging her thighs, soaking her skirt, weighing her down. The wet fabric slipped down, clung to her legs hampering her steps. She plowed on. It was harder to wade through the surging tide than she had imagined. She stopped again to tuck the hem of her skirt in her waistband. Shivering, gasping, she splashed through the numbing salt water and at last drew close to the bird. Now! she thought, and flung out her arms, clutching at the gull. A terrified screech burst from its throat.

Ashly lurched forward, hands outstretched to grip the back of its neck, but its wildly flapping wings knocked them away. She took a step closer and let out a scream as the ground gave way under her feet and she floundered into a hollow. The cold, foaming water eddied about her waist, dragging her down.

Quickly she unzipped her skirt, yanked it down over her legs and kicked it off. She wrung it out as best she could and shook out the folds. Stretching the skirt wide, she flung it over the screaming bird to still its flailing wings.

She braced her back against a tree trunk, gripped the squirming creature and lifted it from the tree. Pressing it close to her chest, she inched through the dark, turbulent waters toward the house.

Intent on freeing the trapped gull, she was unaware of the fast-rising winds. With a sense of shock, she realized they were gusting with renewed vigor and force in the opposite direction from before, whistling through the trees, whipping the water into furious waves. Without warning, as though the clouds had split, rain cascaded down in great gushing torrents. Her hair was plastered to her head and long, dripping strands clung to her eyelids, cheeks, and lips. Rivulets of water streamed down her face.

Ashly shook her head to clear her vision and pushed on through the blinding rain, bent almost double against the hard, driving force of the wind. Gasping, hugging the bundled bird to her breast, she felt like a speck in the vortex of a giant cauldron, spinning faster and faster. The irrational thought occurred to her that though the bodies of dead birds lay all around her, the gull had a right to live. At the same time, like a revelation, it struck her that she herself had the right to live. Terror propelled her onward. Mindlessly, she floundered through the pounding winds and rain, certain that the next instant she would be swept away.

She fixed her numbed gaze on the outside stairway. Only a few more steps and she could grab hold of the railing. As she struggled through the wind-whipped water, dusk waned, giving way to falling darkness. She heard herself screaming and could not stop.

Abruptly her voice was cut off as her mouth filled with brackish saltwater. Choking, sputtering, she stumbled, fell to her knees, spewing out water. She squeezed her eyes shut. Every detail of the terrifying night of the air crash that she had tried so hard to block from her memory flashed through her mind.

Sirens wailed. There were flashing red lights on police cars, amber lights on ambulances. The bridge spanning the dark, ice-clogged river was lined with homeward bound cars, their headlights a string of bright beads, broken, spilling; a jagged white wing-tip slid down into the water; searchlights mounted on trucks were sweeping the river; boats, Coast Guard cutters, fishing and pleasure boats were chopping through the ice-bound waters to reach victims of the crash; she heard voices shouting, crying, pleading, "Here! Over here!" "Oh, God, I'm freezing!" "I can't swim!" Others were thrashing about, clinging to the fuselage, sinking with horrifying speed into the black waters. She was sinking, clutching the seat cushion to her breast. This time she would sink below the surface with the others, to meet her fate as they had done. She heard a voice shouting her name.

"Werner!" she screamed. "I'm here, here!"

Werner, three yards away, turned his head, looked at her with terrified eyes, turned away, swam toward shore. A loop of rope dangled above her head, floated on the water before her. She lunged toward it, but her frozen fingers refused to grab hold. At last she managed to work it over her head, under her arms. The rope tightened, she was being lifted, hauled into a small fishing boat. At the same moment, she saw Werner, sinking down under the swirling waters, never to be seen again.

She heard the crack of a tree limb breaking, falling, the branches snagging her hair. Dark, rushing waters closed over her head.

Chapter 15

Ashly felt something cool press against her lips, then a burning liquid trickled down her throat. Her head ached horribly. Slowly, she floated upward through layers of awareness. From far away she heard Dan's anxious voice.

"Drink this, it'll warm you up."

She opened her eyes. Dan, seated beside her on her bed, an arm around her shoulders, held a sparkling glass of amber liquid to her lips.

"What is it?"

"Cognac." His anxious, worried expression changed to one of intense relief.

"Did the gull survive?"

"Alive and well, rooming with the egret."

His genial expression turned solemn. He set the glass on the nightstand and took her cold hands in his warm ones. Pain contorted his face as he went on in tight, tense tones. "You almost drowned."

She withdrew her hands from his, lifted the glass to her lips and sipped the fiery cognac. Reluctantly she let memory return. "You dragged me in out of the storm, didn't you?"

"You bet I did!" Moisture beaded his forehead and his voice rose in agitation. "You scared the hell out of me. You crazy little fool, what did you think you were doing? Saving the last gull on earth? You could easily have been washed away in the storm surge. Some of the waves were ten or twelve feet high. The island's already been breached in several places. It was sheer luck that I saw you in time." Visibly shaken, he wiped his brow with the back of his hand.

Ashly smiled, touched by his scolding. "And then what happened?"

Dan let out a deep sigh, as though he'd reached the end of his tether. "I carried you inside, tucked you into bed, and here you are."

She gazed down at the pink satin sheet that covered her, sculpting every peak and valley. Her face warmed, pink as the sheet. Dimly she recalled Dan carrying her in his arms, one hand on her cheek, pressing her head snugly against his shoulder; recalled his peeling off her sodden clothes and giving her a brisk rubdown with a huge fluffy towel before tucking the sheet around her. Quietly she said, "Thanks for rescuing me."

Inexplicably, his face clouded and he looked away, avoiding her gaze. "Any time."

Strangely, his voice turned oddly impersonal. He sounded as if rescuing her were all in a day's work, like rescuing an otter, an osprey or a rabbit, and his off-hand manner hurt her.

Tremulously, she asked, "Where's Hallie?"

He shrugged, staring out through the glass doors. "Still a 'big breeze,' but heading inland. The center is dawdling thirty-five miles off the coast. They predict she'll blow herself out by morning."

Through lowered lids, Ashly studied him carefully, trying to figure out his abrupt change in attitude. His manner was cool, his tone remote as he told her of the damage reported on the island, and explained that most of the destruction had been caused by the raging storm tides flooding the land.

She tried to listen, to focus on his words, but her gaze clung to him, troubled, searching. He had risked his life to save her. His expression had been so tender, his hands so gentle when he carried her inside and put her to bed. She had not a doubt in the world he loved her. What had gone wrong?

Abruptly he stood up. "You should eat."

He left and returned shortly bearing a tray with bowls full of steaming clam chowder, crackers, and tea. They ate in an uncomfortable silence and as soon as they had finished, Dan rose to his feet and picked up the tray. "I'd better bed down the animals for the night."

Ashly glanced at the bedside clock. "Dan, it's only seven-fifteen!"

His face took on a closed, set look. "You need to rest after your battle with Hallie. I'll see you in the morning." He leaned down, brushed her brow with his lips and went out.

Disappointment surged through her. Desperately she replayed the scene in her mind. What had she said or done to turn him off so completely? Feeling wretched, she struggled with the problem until sleep overtook her.

Although the rain had stopped, gusting winds continued to howl about the house throughout the night. Ashly drifted in and out of a restless sleep. In the early light of dawn, she was jolted awake by a horrendous crash and the sound of splintering glass.

She jerked bolt upright in bed. At the same instant, as if in slow motion, she saw the soft, feathery boughs of the giant Australian pine that once stood beside the house, toppling, swaying toward her through the shattered glass doors. Horrorstruck, she watched it hurtle downward and with a resounding thud, come to rest. Dripping branches splayed across the foot of her bed.

The wind rushed in, blowing the torn draperies, whirling about the room in gusting fury. Ashly screamed, again and again. It seemed like hours until her door burst open and Dan ran into the room.

His appalled gaze swept past the shattered glass door, the shredded draperies, the sodden pine branches, to Ashly. She sat as though paralyzed in the center of the bed, swathed in the pink satin sheet. Swiftly he crossed to her and gathered her in his arms.

Shivering uncontrollably, she clung to him, burying her head in his shoulder, blotting from sight the ragged draperies, the jagged shards of glass glittering on the bed and floor, the dark green branches of the massive tree. Glass crunched under his feet as he carried her from the room and strode rapidly down the hall, down the wide staircase into the living room. Still holding her tightly in his arms, he sank onto the couch and tipped her face up to his.

Ashen and white-lipped, he asked huskily, "Are you all right?"

Mutely she nodded and nestled closer against his chest, grateful for the shelter of his arms.

With a bone-deep sigh of relief, he kissed the top of her head. "No cuts or bruises?"

Ashly shook her head, and the same instant felt a tremor course through Dan's lean, muscular body. She looked up at him, alarmed. "Are you all right? You're shaking!"

"Shaken," he corrected in dry, hoarse tones. "Do you realize you might have been killed?"

"So could you," she said tremulously. "The tree could just as easily have crashed into your room." At the thought of Dan being killed, her entire being seemed to shatter, as though the sharp slivers from the glass doors pierced her heart. Tears welled in her eyes and rolled down her cheeks.

He kissed them away, murmuring softly, "Don't worry, darling. You're okay. That's all that matters."

"I'm not worried," she quavered. "Just upset, that's all."

His lips curved in a reassuring smile. "There's no further danger. The tree was old and feeble with shallow roots, so instead of weathering the storm, it gave one big sigh and let go. Hallie's still blowing inland."

She looked up at him with a little half-smile. "If Hallie's gone, I'd better be going as well."

Dan stroked her hair soothingly and in authoritative tones said, "You can think about it, but you can't go."

Her eyes widened in question. "No?"

"Definitely not! Fallen trees, downed utility poles, wires across the roads, flooding . . . the roads are impassable. It'll take clean-up crews days to clear away the mess."

Ashly frowned. "I hope not." With more conviction than she felt, she went on, "I'm in a hurry to go back to Washington, to start working again. If I can convince them that I've got it altogether, Palm Air will take me back on six month's probation."

He looked and sounded disgruntled. "Are you sure you're well enough to fly?"

Ashly nodded. Her voice was low and resolute. "Something happened to me out there in the hurricane. Nightmares, anxieties, panic, I thought, it can't get any worse than this, and I made it through. I just have to face the fact that I don't have total control of my life. The reality is that we are all at the mercy of chance. I'm no longer waiting for the trauma to end. It may never end. But the important thing is, now I know I can handle it."

He gazed down at her, a sad and tender light in his eyes. Softly he said, "When you were out there risking your neck for that bird, battling the storm, you were reliving the plane crash, weren't you?"

Ashly nodded, feeling suddenly cold all over.

He let out a long, resigned sigh. "I heard you calling your husband's name, again and again. I knew then that you could never love me as I hoped you would, as I love you." He gazed deeply into her eyes. "I can't compete with a ghost, my love."

As the truth struck home, she stared at him in shocked silence. She jumped up, arms outstretched, crying out, "Dan, you don't understand."

With an air of defeat, he said softly, "Oh, but I do understand. You wanted no commitments because you're still in love with your husband. I can tell by the way you said his name."

She drew back from him, staring up into his face in shock. With grim conviction he went on, "I can't deny the evidence of my own ears."

Looking up at him, tears staining her cheeks, she felt all the knotted emotions within her begin to unravel. For the first time, she found she could speak of her past without feeling the strangling sensation that closed her throat, choked off her breath.

"Dan, the truth is, I felt so terribly guilty that I'd survived when so many had died. And I felt I could have tried harder to save Werner, but I didn't. Right from the start, when we had trouble gaining altitude, I had this gut feeling we'd never make it. You do understand that, don't you?"

Solemnly he nodded. "You were on the flight crew?"

"No," she said miserably. "Still, I could have helped with emergency procedures, but everything happened so fast—"

"Ashly, I read the newspaper account. It said all those who died inside the plane were killed by the impact. So all your emergency procedures would have been useless. And you couldn't possibly have saved your husband's life."

"I know," she said softly. She lowered her eyes, unable to meet his gaze. "I saw him, called out to him."

He placed the palms of his hands on her cheeks, turning her head to face him. Very softly, he said, "You've never stopped loving him, have you?"

She ran her tongue over dry lips. How could she tell him the secret she had locked away for so long in a dark corner of her soul? She had to try! In quavering tones she began:

"Werner was going to a business meeting in Tampa. I was traveling with him, going to visit Jessamine and Ted—" She stopped, shaking her head. "I don't think I can tell you, Dan."

He took her hands in his, stroking the backs with his thumbs. "Just tell me about visiting Jessamine."

She swallowed hard, and went on. "Jessamine had been begging me to visit her, but Werner never wanted me to leave him. He said I was gone too much as it was, flying for Palm Air. Then when he had to go to Tampa on business, he could think of no reason why I couldn't go along."

Dan's smoky blue eyes filled with sympathy and understanding. But she knew he didn't understand, not really.

She plunged on, hating the way her voice shook. "After the plane went down, I felt guilty about the passengers dying, but I felt even worse when—when Werner—died."

Dan, holding her hands tightly in his, gave them a comforting squeeze. She took a deep breath. "I felt even worse because—because more than once, I had wished him dead."

Dan's tanned features mirrored incredulous disbelief. His hands stroking hers, stilled.

Her last shred of control deserted her as she burst out, "I was going to divorce Werner. I wanted to be free of him. I never intended just to *visit* Jessamine. I was going to *stay* with her—until I found a place of my own." She covered her face with her hands. Sobs shook her slender shoulders.

Dan put his arms around her and gathered her close against his chest, smoothing away her tears, murmuring, "Ashly, Ashly, darling, what an intolerable burden of guilt you've been carrying."

Her throat ached with the effort of speaking out, but she forced herself to go on. "I thought I could forget, but it's impossible."

Dan stroked her hair, resting his chin against her forehead. "What an awful man he must have been."

Ashly shook her head. "He could be the most charming man in the world." She looked up at Dan with a little half-smile on her lips. "Werner fooled me completely. I had no intention of being fooled again. No intention of falling in love, with you or anyone else." She sighed deeply, and with it all the bitterness seemed to drain from her soul.

"Werner was all a woman could want in a man—when he was sober. When he wasn't, well,—" Her voice broke, but she forced herself to go on. "All his hidden hostilities and aggressions boiled over. He had to attack someone, and I was there."

Dan's eyes flashed fire. "Why didn't Jessamine and Ted come to your defense then, when you needed them?"

"They never knew. I kept the dark side of my marriage from Jessamine as long as I could. I didn't want her to worry about me. I wanted her to be happy." A rueful smile twisted her lips. "In the early days I was willing to do anything to save our marriage. I never could accept failure, you see. But when Jessamine kept begging me to come to Sanibel, I was determined to go, with or without Werner. His business trip just made it easier. As soon as we landed, I was going to tell him it was all over between us." She let out a despairing sigh. "By that time, Jessamine knew our marriage had failed. Although I'd kept the unpleasant facts from her, Ted paid us a surprise visit in Washington, saw the bruises on my arm and guessed the rest. Naturally, he told Jessamine. They threatened to come to Washington and take me away if I didn't leave Werner." Her lips curved in a small grin. "So now you can understand why they're super-protective and why they're overdoing it."

Dan nodded. "I thought it was because you'd lost your husband."

A brittle laugh escaped her. "Perhaps you judged my marriage by your own."

Gently he said, "My marriage is like a book I read long ago and loved, but I've no need to read it again. It belongs to the past." He smiled gently at her. "Don't you know that a once-happily-married-widower makes the best husband?"

Realizing she was gazing up at him, with all the love and admiration she felt for him shining in her eyes, she rose from the couch and clutching the pink sheet snugly about her, she said quietly, "We've said it all, Dan. It's time for me to go."

The corners of his mouth quirked, and she had the unsettling feeling he was laughing at her. Confused, she said, "I shouldn't have come back. You and the animals would have weathered Hallie just fine without my help."

An unholy light glistened in his eyes. "It's an ill wind that blows nobody good. Just think, if Hallie hadn't blown in, you'd never have come back to me."

She felt a faint fluttering in the region of her heart, like a fallen bird coming to life. She gave a vehement shake of her head. "It was the causeway. Hurricane or sunshine, no matter. It was my lifeline to you. No way could I drive across it!"

He was gazing at her sorrowfully. "But now you're ready to fly again. You want your freedom, just like my wildlife friends."

Standing before him, the pink satin sheet draped about her, Ashly gazed at him from eyes filled with wonder. A great singing sensation began in her heart. She took a deep breath. "Yes, Dan, I'm ready to fly again. But I'm not going to." She tossed her hair back over her shoulders, lifting her head in an independent tilt.

He looked at her intently, his head cocked to one side. "What, then? What *are* you going to do?"

Her eyes glistened with anticipation and hope. "You've shown me another way of life, one with purpose and meaning. The work we're doing at the Center really matters to me." She took another deep breath, bracing herself for whatever was to come. "I'm going to follow the Pied Piper of Sanibel, if he still wants—"

Before she finished speaking, Dan jumped to his feet and pulled her into his arms, crushing her against his chest, his cheek pressing into the softness of her hair, his lips warm against her ear. In a voice husky with emotion, he murmured, "My darling, I've loved you from the day I saved you from drowning in the Gulf."

The words, "You did not *save* me!" trembled on her

lips. She closed them firmly, reveling in Dan's words as he went on. "The sweetest thing I've ever known is loving you."

She drew back, gazing up into his face, her eyes misting. "Dan, you've given me the courage to listen to my heart."

Huskily, he murmured, "You are my only love, now and forever." His arms tightened around her, his lips closed over hers in a long, ardent kiss. Gradually Ashly became aware that they were enveloped in a peaceful calm, unbroken by the sounds of menacing winds and rain. In the still, clear silence, she heard a songbird trill.

Arms entwined about each other, they strolled through the glass doors onto the deck. Gazing out over the serene Gulf waters, Ashly saw that the storm tides had begun to recede, and Dan's sturdy cabin stood staunchly amid the devastation that surrounded them. In quiet wonder, she said, "The destruction isn't as bad as I thought."

Dan, smiling down at her, hugged her close to his side. "Nothing is as bad as we think. We'll clear away the storm damage and make a new start, build our lives together."

Gently he turned her within the circle of his arms as the sun rose around them.